RX JUPITER SAVE US

By
WARD MOORE

I0541446

ARMCHAIR FICTION
PO Box 4369, Medford, Oregon   97501-0168

*For more information about Armchair Books and products, visit our
website at…*

www.armchairfiction.com

Or email us at…

armchairfiction@yahoo.com

THE COMING OF FREEDOM...

It was a strange world, where absolutism reigned without violence, and rebels were sure that—once their strength became known—the rulers would abdicate power gracefully. But Green Ed-jo, Jovian freak, knew differently—and saw very little desirability between the tyranny of the Plotbureau...and the chaos of the Readers.

Ed-jo and his allies knew that if man wasn't free to choose, he wasn't free at all. And if so, it was better to be superseded by machines.

FOR A COMPLETE SECOND NOVEL, TURN TO PAGE 103

CAST OF CHARACTERS

GREEN ED-JO
He believed in compromise—but that compromise would not disdain the use of force when necessary.

NKA WILL-JIM
His bits of ancient knowledge helped play a pivotal role in showing the way things really were.

MULLA FERA-LIZ
She had two sets of arms with six fingers on each hand. Just what a girl needed to get things done!

NORE LIL-ISA
An exotic beauty with Ebony skin. Would Green Ed-Jo ever come to see this world as she did?

YOHSEN JOHANS
He was strong in mind and body—and he had carried the secrets of the Readers to a chosen few.

NIELS SVEN-YORN
This respected elder was one of the many Readers placed in Lank to help build the rebellion.

CHAPTER ONE

THE SUPE in the Immigration Service—an arm designed, as the name implies, to prevent immigration—and Green Ed-jo, aged seven, stepped out of the official 'copter onto the roof of the Beaural Building in Lank. Two proles, like themselves dressed in thermo-suits for outdoor wear, emerged from a stairwell and guided the 'copter to a parking ramp. Ed-jo followed the supe down an escalator to the floor below, passing patrolling proles who, like all guards except those on the planetary exmosphliers, were completely unarmed.

A telespeaker, evidently operated by an electronic eye, ordered courteously, "Please give the password for today."

"Quantum," answered the supe, without breaking his stride.

"Thank you," the telespeaker called after them.

A great, latchless door opened gently, murmuring monotonously, "Beaural Building, Beaural Building," and shut behind them, terminating its statement on the sixth "Buil." The even, odorless atmosphere of the air-conditioning reminded them they were still dressed for outdoors; they halted and shrugged out of the thermo-suits, dropping them in a conveniently placed disposer.

"Thank you," the apparatus rippled.

They entered a waiting elevator. "Four sixty," directed the supe. The door slid shut and almost instantly opened again. "Floor four hundred and sixty," said the speaker, "Thank you."

They rode a silent conveyor along a quietly lit corridor, repeated the password to another telespeaker when they came to the break, which let them cross the conveyor moving in the opposite direction, and stopped before a blank wall. "Quantum," began the supe. "Szuki Fred-hara, Immigration, with a controversial subject."

"One moment, please," said the wall. For the first time Ed-jo felt scared and alone.

"You may come in; the Director will see you," said the wall, opening into a room. At the far end, the Director lay on a couch looking up at a telescreen fixed at the angle most comfortable to the reclining position. Two other screens were on opposing walls. An Orsogian robot, its antenna stiffly erect, tentacles hanging down, looking like an ancient floormop—as pictured in that priceless archaeological work recently excavated in the ruins of Old Chik, *Sears*—stood behind its master, whose lips moved as the wall closed behind Ed-jo and the supe.

"This is highly irregular, Szuki, practically controversial." The pettish voice, amplified, came from the walls as the Director continued to whisper. "Personal interviews are clumsy and inefficient, not versive at all. Can't understand why you didn't contact in the usual manner."

"This is a controversial case, Your Honor."

"I should think so. I suppose this incompletely-developed humanoid tried to slip in from Mars or Venus. Obviously a decoy, Szuki; you picked him up and let his mature accomplices get by you." In his agitation the director lifted his head a full three inches off the couch, just like one of the lower grades who were not granted full relief from physical activity.

"This is not a humanoid, Your Honor, but a terrestrial citizen, Green Ed-jo."

The director relaxed. "Ah. An impermissible. I still see no excuse for this distasteful personal proximity. The social adjuster will reclassify him for you."

"He is permissibly born, Your Honor. I thought his name might recall the case to you; it was a notorious one."

"Information has miles of electronic memory banks. I do not tax my own. You would be advised to do the same, Szuki."

"Yes, Your Honor. It only stuck in my mind because it was mentioned so often on *Human Interest Stories* before that program was discontinued as too suggestive of the archaic newscasts. This is the child born on Jupiter, of the organizers (j g) Green Jon-enry and Green Mary-en who secured a reproduction certificate (Class B, not renewable nor transferable, limited to one child and good until revoked) before taking up their assignment which was overseeing the collection, slaughter, dehydration, packing and shipping of Jovian goochs."

AT THE WORD "goochs" Ed-jo's homesickness overwhelmed him.

The penguinlike, avian bipeds—the aboriginal Jovians—had been his nurses, companions, friends and mentors from birth. He thought with fierce nostalgia of the warm, feathery comfort of their touch, of the hundred services they performed in the degravited area—the cosie—his parents had been forced to confine themselves to escape the tremendous gravitational pull of Jupiter. The boy bit his lips to keep from betraying emotion before these hateful Earth-people.

The director's eyes turned toward him, but the expression of extreme boredom did not change. "Jupiter, ay? Irregular, even if permissible. Well, tune the WBI and have his punch-card fed to the Central Troubleshooter. What do you suppose machines are for? Really, I wonder if you hadn't better feed your own card to a review-board; failure to make such an elementary decision seems to suggest need for reclassification, or even a Happy Despatch."

"His punch-card is defective; Central Troubleshooter will not respond to it."

"Nonsense! Preposterous...there hasn't been a defective punch-card since the Plotbureau Ok'd automatic rectifiers on the WBI vitatistics, which crosschecks with Information and the perpetual census. Don't try to cover up your inefficiency with such transparent untruths."

"As Your Honor knows," said Szuki in a leisurely manner, as though he were beginning to enjoy the conversation—now that the responsibility was resting on his superior—"the initial item on all punch-cards is the date of birth and all the relevant statistics. This is followed by the serial-number of the parents' permission to reproduce, thus opening a line of cross-reference leading back into the archives clear to the beginnings of civilization—to that glorious day when everyone on earth was fingerprinted and recorded without exception. If, on the other hand, no serial-number appears, the subject is automatically classified as a prole, and no certificate of reproduction is ever issued to him or her."

"Thon," the director murmured in correction; "ever issued to thon. Ancient history, all of it. What's the point of telling me stuff I could have gotten more pleasantly by tuning Information?"

"Only this, Your Honor: the third item is the juvenry assignment; then the tentative classifications and reclassifications; the permanent one; and the preversty assignment at the age of six. Green Ed-jo's card lacks reference to a juvenry and is without a classification since that is made in one. He is not only unclassified—*he cannot be classified!*"

There was a pause. "I feel the need of a stimulant," whispered the director.

His robot immediately reached out a tentacle toward the wall. After a short interval, a round opening appeared into which the tentacle was thrust, withdrawing a small lucite flagon. The wall closed as the robot broke the seal on the flask with another tentacle, and placed it against the director's lips with a third.

"Very inconvenient," he gasped, after the robot had removed the empty flagon, produced a fiber cloth, wiped his lips and discarded both cloth and flagon in the disposer. "Very inconvenient. Can't give it orders when it's holding something against my mouth; have to take it all at once, even if it chokes me. You'd think the Orsogians would improve their robots or else the televentors would come up with an attachment to solve the problem.

"Hum. Now as to this unclassified boy. Hum. An immediate Happy Despatch would settle everything, but no review-board will recommend one while his punch-card shows no assignment, and therefore no unprofitable ineffi-ciency."

"And he cannot be assigned without the required term at a preversty." prompted the supe.

"Nor sent to a preversty without a classification. It seems an insuperable problem."

"Exactly why I brought it to Your Honor in this slightly irregular fashion."

"In this very irregular fashion. Hum. It seems to me…"

There was silence while Ed-jo, bored, hungry, uncomfortable and nervous, fidgeted.

"Get me Information," ordered the director suddenly.

The two wall telescreens lit up, and a section of Information—a series of wires, tubes and condensers—appeared on them.

"Are there still subnormals?" inquired the director.

"Please rephrase your question," said Information.

"Of all the inefficient devices! Oh, very well. Are these humans under the age of—" he broke off to look at Ed-jo

"—say ten, whose tests indicate the impossibility of benefit from attendance at a preversty?"

Several tubes glowed; a light somewhere in the interior of Information flashed on and off. "Your answer is yes."

"Ha," exclaimed the director. "Ha. And what is done with these subnormals?"

"Please rephrase your question," admonished Information.

Sputtering that the prudery of machines was beyond all belief, the director complied, using more decorous language.

"Your answer is that such citizens are considered mutants."

"Mutants," repeated the director. "Of course. Deviations from the norm. Perfect logic. His eyes moved back to Information. "How are mutants conditioned for service?"

"Mutants are inadvisable material for preversities," said Information; "due to individualistic or un-uniform response. They are therefore assigned to tradeskills until the age of eighteen, when they are assigned just as though they were classified as proles—unless in the meantime they reveal disabilities indicating the desirability of a Happy Despatch."

"Thank you," said the director. "That is all."

"Thank *you*," responded Information, fading out.

THE SUPE cleared his throat nervously. "I should have mentioned that the boy has a definite physical disability. He can fly."

"I can *not!*" protested Ed-jo shrilly.

"Perhaps 'soar' is the more exact word. The boy can soar. After his—um—parents—"

"Szuki! Need you be so obscene?"

"Pardon me, Your Honor. The fact remains however. Having been born on Jupiter, he was never placed in a juvenry but remained in unhealthy proximity to—um— Green Mary-en and Jon-enry until the moment of debarkation at the Lank spaceport. Well, after the Greens—organizers, (j g)—were cleared for re-entry, I was confronted with the problem of this unclassified boy. I asked him to follow me, which he did quite normally in the comparatively-confined space of the exmosphlier; but once unhampered by the other passengers, as we reached the ground his steps became great leaps, taking him eight or ten feet into the air."

"I couldn't help it," interrupted Ed-jo sullenly; "the ground sort of had springs in it. Not like outside at home, but like in the cosie. How did I know the ground was degravitated?"

"Hmm, hmmm," said the director. "Conceived, gestated and born on Jupiter. His density must be that of the inhabitants—if there are any inhabitants but goochs. Undoubtedly unfit for terrestrial conditions. No question but that a review-board will recommend a Happy Despatch."

"Don't want a Happy Despatch; want something to eat."

"Not want a Happy Despatch? But everyone wants a Happy Despatch. If they didn't, there would be too many people. We look forward to it all our lives; it's our reward and culmination."

"Don't want—"

"You don't realize what you're saying. Why, when a review board prescribes a Happy Despatch, the recipient is the subject of congratulations. For a week he is a—well, we have no word for it in the modern tongue. I disapprove of the affectation of archaic expressions, but if I may permit myself this once, for a week you are a god. All the privileges of the upper classifications are insignificant compared with undergoing the Happy Despatch. No exertion of any kind is necessary; even breathing; is assisted by mechanical means and the subject lies in a stupor of relaxed bliss. All the carefully cultivated inhibitions are put aside. You do what you want, think what you please. Eat for enjoyment, drink

11

for pleasure, mate for lust. At the end of the week stupefied with excesses, you sink into a glorious, drugged sleep full of beautiful dreams."

"Don't want to sleep," persisted Ed-jo obstinately; "want something to eat."

"You are one of the most controversial citizens I've ever met," said the director irritably. "Information." The screen lit. "What of subjects who don't want a Happy Despatch when it is recommended?"

"Inadmissible hypothesis. Humans are conditioned to accept cybernetic suggestions unquestioningly, because machines are constructed to serve humanity."

"Suppose the subject weren't conditioned?"

A red light obscured Information's insides. "Beep-beep-beep."

"Paradox," muttered Szuki. "No possible reply. Everyone is intensively conditioned; information can't deal with non-existents."

"Really?" said the director coldly. "Your talent for discovering the obvious is phenomenal." He turned back to Information. "Suppose the human were aberrant, disloy? How could he be compelled, for his own and society's good?"

"No human may use force against another," answered Information, "or direct a machine to use force against a human. Mankind survives because, having come to the edge of destruction through the use of violence, it has permanently given it up, conditioning itself firmly against its use. Force was always inefficient; conditioned obedience is efficient. No one thinks of disobeying the order of his superior, or of the machines constructed for the good of the human race."

The director grunted. "Thank you; that is all. I think, Szuki, a tradeskill for mutants is definitely indicated."

CHAPTER TWO

GREEN ED-JO'S ten years at Lank Tradeskill would seem monstrous torture to us today, a routine of dull, unrelieved boredom. But then, all existence Before Freedom is drab and deadening compared with our world of AF.

Monstrous and deadening as it was however, the tradeskill represented joyous activity contrasted with the preversity. Though the curricula was theoretically the same, the mutants were so varied and unpredictable in their reactions it was difficult to persuade them to spend their entire waking days looking raptly at television screens, as the normal students did. Consequently much time was used in "fieldwork"—a pedagogic survival ignored at the preversity, and repugnant to a civilization admiring immobility and reserving activity contemptuously for its lowest classifications.

So mutants who weren't completely apathetic became self reliant and inquiring to a degree unknown to other proles, or the upper classifications, as they explored, not the pictures of industry on radiowaves, but the actual operations themselves. They took the elevators from the hundredth floor where the tradeskill was located, down to the fiftieth and lower floors where the base of the Beaural Building broadened out to its ultimate area to accommodate the machineshops, refineries and factories housed there.

Growing older, they explored still more unusual places. They went deep into the earth to the caverns where the cyclotrons produced power not only for the city of Lank, but for a share of the immense surplus transmitted by radio to the robots, copters, intercontinentals, and mining and drilling machines far away. They even went entirely outside the building—many proles spent entire lives under one roof—to

13

visit others housing foundries, rolling mills, or the cybernets: the machines determining and directing practically all human activity, and the even more complex ones which designed and then coordinated production, gearing it to terrestrial needs and export demands.

Recalling the humiliation of his introduction to Earth, Ed-jo was careful not to betray his superiority over gravity to the tradeskill's strawbs and supes—the organizer never appeared in person, but presumably viewed all that went on from the 377th floor, where she was infrequently consulted. However, when he felt free of the presence of adults, Ed-jo demonstrated his disability for the pleasure of his particular friends, Nka Will-jim, a cyclops, and Mulla Fera-liz, who had two pair of arms, with six fingers on each of her four hands—which made a problem of the otherwise simple business of calling on the dispensor for a thermo-suit to wear outside the building.

At first, the advantage was all theirs, for Ed-jo was limited to showing how he could apparently climb a straight wall without handholds, or rise from floor to ceiling and descend gently. Fera-liz, walking on four hands—or combing her hair, eating a hydroponic apple, spinning a top and thumbing her nose simultaneously was vastly more spectacular.

Will-jim's talents were of an entirely different order: he had a photographic memory. In other historical periods this would have been an invaluable asset; at a time when retention of anything beyond elementary vocabulary was considered atavism, it was simply a curiosity. There seemed to be no point in remembering facts or principles when the answer to any problem, properly formulated, could be gotten instantly by tuning Information. As sheer entertainment however, Will-jim's ability to recall what had appeared on the telescreen—down to the most trivial detail—a day, week or month before was as fascinating as his single, centered eye.

It was only when the tradeskill made excursions beyond the city of Lank that Ed-jo was able to relax the constant control he kept on his legs, to simulate what was—to him— the hobbling stride of the Earth-born. Once the helicopters had lifted them from the roof and borne them beyond the hills surrounding Lank, out into the pale desert or the rugged canyons, he was free—except for concealment from the strawb in charge—to sprint across the ground in great leaps, to hop across wide gullies or bound over the tops of all but the very tallest trees.

As the supes of the tradeskill had long noted unhappily, many of the mutants—in addition to their characteristic poor response to conditioning—were particularly deficient in accepting the agoraphobia which was such an important factor in Beaural civilization. A normal, well-adjusted man hesitated to go from floor to floor, suffered painful anxiety at the thought of going outside a building, and was terrified at the prospect of visiting the wild country beyond Lank—even, as in the case of the tradeskill officials, when it was part of their assignment. The mutants, on the other hand, actually seemed to enjoy the wild country which stretched for thousands of miles toward the cities of Chik and Nork, a vast primeval wilderness broken only by outposts—places of sad exile, to which assignment was dreaded, and usually preceded request for a review-board almost always prescribing a Happy Despatch—where were mined the raw materials for the factories, mills and powerhouses of the cities.

Except for those once designated by the ancient and outmoded terms, "moron", "cretin", and so forth, who in spite of their docility were early given a Happy Despatch, the mutants appeared more at ease among the rocks and brush and ruins of individual buildings (dating from the time before all activities were concentrated in the cities, and food had

been raised—incredibly—directly on the surface of the earth)
than they were in the tightly enclosed safety of the buildings.

WHILE THE strawb clung to the comparative comfort of
the helicopter's interior, Ed-jo, Will-jim and Fera-liz
gamboled and explored without the slightest thought of the
ostensible reason for the outing which was to contrast the
order and efficiency of life under the Plotbureau with what it
had been in the mad scramble of the Dark Ages, or the slow
and painful reconstruction in the period before the Bureau
took over. Instead of absorbing this edifying lesson, they
threw rocks at wild rabbits, cowered helplessly into whatever
shelter they could seize when a herd of bison pounded past,
or ran in shrieking fright at the sight of a bear.

It was a bear that finally forced Ed-jo's disability on the
notice of the strawb. Fera-liz had been climbing along the
underside of a sycamore limb, an understandably simple acro-
batic feat for anyone with six limbs. Will-jim, usually content
to leave the more spectacular athletic trials to the others, this
time had an impulse to imitate Fera-liz. While they looked
on, shouting ironic encouragement, he struggled up the trunk
and out onto the limb. Suddenly the bear was at the foot of
the tree, standing erect, his forepaws resting on the bark, his
long muzzle sniffing curiously upward.

"It's all right," whispered Ed-jo, "we'll just have to wait till
he gets tired and goes away."

The bear was, unfortunately, of a different species from
those to which they were accustomed. Slowly, gracefully,
digging in his claws, he began to climb. Surveying the
situation calmly from his perch, Will-jim called down, "Run
toward the copter, Liz; make as much noise as you can.
Throw a rock at him, Jo, without attracting him toward you."

They obeyed, but the bear refused to be decoyed. Will-jim
edged further out; the bear put an exploratory paw on the

crotch where it joined the trunk. Fera-liz was nowhere in sight, but Ed-jo knew that by the time she reached the copter, explained the situation, and got the strawb to bring the machine to Will-jim's rescue, it would be too late.

Will-jim cautiously moved out still further, to where the limb was unquestionably just a branch—an extremely supple one. Lazily, the bear followed. "OK," shouted Ed-jo, "here I come."

He felt a surge of well-being as his feet left the ground. There was no room for him on the branch, nor time for him to pause there; the bear was very close. He was not sure what would happen when Will-jim's weight was added to his own, but he grabbed the cyclops around the waist and they descended to the ground. Ed-jo came down at a faster speed than he was used to, but one, which could certainly not be called falling. Then they ran, leaving the bear, with a look of puzzled injury, staring into empty space.

The copter had already risen to rescue Will-jim, so that the strawb witnessed Ed-jo's jump. She was much disturbed. Such anachronistic muscular displays betokened maladjustment, insecurity, overcompensation, aggression, and all the other factors incompatible with Beaural Civilization. Shaking her head, she predicted a review board before he was a month on his first assignment.

THAT ASSIGNMENT came from the social adjuster when Green Ed-jo was just turned eighteen, along with those of Nka Will-jim and Mulla Fera-liz.

The cybernetic voice spoke from the telescreen, "…maintenance crew Lank one-oh-eight." Adding explanatorily, "P7 mutants (physical divergences from the established norm, minus responsiveness to conditioning, notable bodily activity) are recorded as satisfactory in extraurban labor. Unless a controversial disposition appears, there is a negative probability of reassignment or review-board for an average of four years, sixty-five days, thirteen and a quarter hours. These three P7 mutants will remove immediately to Prok quarters B85A on the eighty-fifth floor of the Metro Building. Since you will have to leave your room, floor and building, you will receive the password for today by stepping up to the screen for proper identification…"

"Well," said Will-jim, blinking his single eye, "at least we're going to be together."

Fera-liz snapped eight fingers with a crackling noise. "There was no marital assignment attached."

Will-jim looked disgusted. "I guess that's what the cybernet meant by minus responsiveness to conditioning. You've been told often enough that mutants get no marital status before twenty."

"That's right," said Fera-liz. "Gosh. Two years. Sometimes a girl gets an urge."

"You'll probably be assigned some prole who can barely move," suggested Ed-jo unsympathetically. "Compensate for your extra arms, you know."

"What's the difference?" asked Will-jim. "Proles can't get a certificate to reproduce anyway."

"I wish I'd get a tall fellow with dark curly hair," murmured Fera-liz dreamily. "I'd just love to run twenty four fingers through it."

The password for that day being "dianetic," they ordered thermo-suits, not bothering to indicate a special for Fera-liz, since she would have no occasion to use more than one pair of arms on the trip. The suits were delivered almost instantly through the servadors: after putting them on they took an elevator to the roof and a jeecar along the bileway to the Metro Building. "I think this password business is simply silly," announced Fera-liz, "and so are all those guards standing around."

"Survivals are always silly; if they aren't silly, then they aren't survivals, but merely a custom which is changing its form or function," said Will-jim pedantically.

IN THE PROLE quarters of the Metro Building they met the other three members of the maintenance crew. "We've never worked with mutants before," said Ching Mei-lu, who had a habit of tossing her head, "I'm thrilled. Can you see just as well with one eye?" she asked Will-jim.

"As well as what?" he countered, "When you have two eyes the focus of one corrects the other. When you have one eye there is no need of correction. I see as well as I need."

If Will-jim had meant to reprove her, the reproof was ineffectual. "And four arms. Don't some of them get in your way?" Without waiting for an answer, she turned to Ed-jo. "What a funny color for hair! It's sort of yellow, isn't it?"

"At one time," explained Will-jim, "as you will no doubt recall from your conditioning, men were divided into physically-distinctive groups. Some of these had light-colored hair and eyes, which, for some reason not clear to us, they cherished as a symbol of superiority over the majority of men who, like us, had full, natural pigmentation. These whites—as they were miscalled—for actually they were a yellowish pinky-gray—demonstrated their superiority by robbing, murdering and enslaving those of a different complexion whenever they could. However this deficiency of pigmentation is biologically recessive, so that it has gradually disappeared, even though traces of it crop up occasionally in freaks like Ed-jo."

"What's the good of remembering all that tiresome stuff the way you do?" asked Fera-liz. "When we want to know any of those silly things all we have to do is tune Information."

"We haven't been on this job long ourselves," explained Yohsen Jo-hans. We were only assigned a few months ago from the preversity; the three old members of the crew were reassigned yesterday."

"We think they got a review-board and that almost certainly means a Happy Despatch for extraurban workers!" exclaimed Mei-lu. "Of course they're enjoying themselves tremendously right now, but I just can't help feeling a little sad—"

"How you chatter on," interrupted Narc Lil-isa, whose black skin, much darker than the others', had a glowing quality Ed-jo had never noticed in a girl before.

"Lil-isa is right," said Jo-hans; "sometimes remarks we know are just silly can be considered controversial."

"Oh, don't mind us," said Will-jim. "Mutants don't condition well."

Jo-hans gave him a sharp look, but the cyclop's eye stared innocently back. "Well," he muttered at last, "I suppose you'll want to know about the job. Most proles detest going out of the building into the wild country and doing different work each time, but we sort of like it. Not that we haven't been conditioned to prefer regular routine but..." his voice trailed off uncertainly, as though he had said more than he had intended, and didn't quite know how to retract his words.

"We don't care much for monotony," said Ed-jo. "We're atavars, you know—throwbacks to the days when everybody worked outside the building where they lived."

JO-HANS kept his eyes down. "You probably know how Lank gets its water. Three aqueducts run east and north to tap rivers, and there is a short conveyor for converted sea-water."

"I would have thought water from the ocean would make the aqueducts obsolete," remarked Ed-jo.

Jo-hans was silent, but Will-jim said, "It's one of those things. Beaural civilization is full of contradictions—"

"Oh dear," protested Fera-liz; "if you're going to start talking like a conditioning cybernet again, I'm going to sleep."

"No cybernet ever said anything so controversial," stated Jo-hans grimly. "I'd think I'd rather not listen to the rest of what you were going to say."

"I think we can trust these people," put in Lil-isa gently. "Go on, Will-jim."

"I'd be willing to bet, for instance, that plans were drawn up centuries ago for more converters to replace the freshwater aqueducts, and the Plotbureau has never done a thing to start the replacement-process."

"The replacement-process would have gone on by itself once the teleplanner made the blueprints," argued Ed-jo. "What you mean is that the Bureau actually stopped the cycle somewhere."

"That doesn't make sense," objected Mei-lu. "The Bureau exists because it directs mankind with the utmost efficiency."

There was a silence. Finally Jo-hans said in his heavy, slow way, "These are controversial thoughts."

"Not mine," said Fera-liz. "I wasn't even thinking about such dull stuff. Do you have a marital assignment, Jo-hans?"

Jo-hans blushed and shook his head. "I was supposed to have, but a ruling by the social adjuster postponed marital status for extra urban workers till the age of twenty-five."

"Oh no! wailed Fera-liz. "In seven years I'll be a—what's the archaic word, Will-jim?"

"Old maid. What difference does it make?"

"You wouldn't understand. Sometimes a girl gets an urge."

"Look," said Jo-hans nervously, "about the job. The fresh water aqueducts are very ancient, dating way back to the Dark Ages. You'll hardly believe this, but they were originally made of steel. Naturally, in the course of centuries they have been repaired so often their entire length has been replaced, first by duramagnesium—which is hardly used at all, nowadays—and finally by bessemite."

"Honestly," commented Mei-lu, "it's you who talk like a cybernet. It's all so simple," she went on, addressing herself to Fera-liz. "When something goes wrong on the aqueducts or the seawater conveyor, the electronic impulses running along them are interrupted. This naturally activates a troubleshooter—"

"Not the big social troubleshooter connected to the WBI and the loyalty checks, but a little mechanical troubleshooter concerned only with our job," explained Lil-isa in her soft voice, which reminded Ed-jo so illogically of the half-forgotten warmth and comfort of the goochs. He was aware of a perfectly irrational pleasure in knowing she had no marital assignment.

"Which locates the exact spot affected by teletectors, which also show whether it's a leak or a failure in the syphons or the pumping system—"

"But it's usually a stoppage in the conveyor," interrupted Jo-hans. "Telemeters measure the replacement if one is called for and the piece is fabricated to their specifications."

"Sounds fully automatic and mechanical so far," said Ed-jo.

"Not entirely; as you'll see after you're on the job awhile. Anyway it isn't mechanical from then on. The replacement is loaded on a freightcopter, since they can't use rockepults the way they do for raw materials—"

"Why not? asked Fera-liz without much interest.

"Because the rockepults only work between fixed points," said Will-jim. "Anybody can see that with one eye. There wouldn't be any point in setting up a rockepult terminal every time the pipe had to be repaired—and if there were they'd need copters to do it."

"Well," continued Jo-hans, "we go out in the copter with the replacement, the tools and the machines and make the repairs. That's all there is to it. Most proles hate it because the hours are odd and irregular."

"I think I'm going to like it," said Ed-jo.

CHAPTER THREE

THE CREW got their first call the next day, just before Nightfeed. They ate cold rations on the freightcopter, sitting wedged in by machinery. "I like this," announced Fera-liz. "It's fun to eat this way."

"In very ancient times it was frequently done for pleasure, and went by the obsolete word, 'picnic', among the savages who practiced the custom," Will-jim told her.

"It's considered one of the most disagreeable features of the job," said Jo-hans. "Leaving the security of the building is bad enough, but to miss Nightfeed—when every prole in Lank is eating at the same time—is supposed to be the unhappiest deprivation of all."

"Well, I still think it's fun," insisted Fera-liz.

The copter set down in a spot where no trees—only heavy brush—grew guided there by a course set by the coordinated calculations of the teletector, troubleshooter and several other machines concerned in the repair of the aqueduct. The searchlights, drawing power from the generators of far-off Lank, were quickly set up; the new bessemite section unloaded; and the cyberwelders rolled into place. Beyond the brilliant lights focused on the spot under repair, the desert stretched out in blackness.

But not quite total blackness. A sky full of stars was visible to Ed-jo as soon as his eyes became accustomed to the dark. "What are you looking at?" asked Lil-isa, her soft voice close to him.

"Up there," he said. "One of those stars in Jupiter; I was born on it."

He could hear the startled indrawing of her breath. "You were *what?*"

"I was born on Jupiter; it says so on my punch-card. Just for fun I got all the dope from Information. Seems there was a slip-up somewhere; anyway I'm the only one ever happened."

"I can hardly believe it," whispered Lil-isa.

"Why not? My mother and father had a certificate. I'm permissibly born," he added with some pride.

"I didn't mean *that*. I—well, I can't explain just what I did mean, right now. Tell me, can you point to Jupiter?"

"Afraid I never got too much out of conditioning, especially when the cybernet was going on about astronomy and the spectroscope and all that," Ed-jo confessed. "Those celestial charts moving around—they made me dizzy."

Lil-isa laughed. "It's better to learn out of books, if you really want to know something—instead of just being conditioned for the sake of convenience."

"Books?"

"Reading."

"Both words are familiar. I hear them often on the telescreen, but not the way you've used them."

"That's what your friend Will-jim would call another of the contradictions of Beaural civilization. Semantics outlawed the 'figure of speech' centuries ago, and its use is considered a controversial sign; yet the telerecords are full of metaphor. They still speak of 'reading meaning into things' and 'compiling books' though both the verb and the noun have officially disappeared long ago. Perhaps you may find out that they have other than metaphorical meanings sometime. Meanwhile, up there, where my finger is pointing, is Jupiter."

"Ah," murmured Ed-jo, "it's bright."

"And there—over there—is Isha, or Venus. It's smaller, much smaller, but much brighter."

"Oh, Venus. Yes," said Ed-jo indifferently. "That's where the humanoids are so backward, isn't it?"

"Oh! Oh you—you *patriot!* 'Humanoids'. 'Backward'. And mutants are supposed to be hard to condition!"

Jo-hans' voice called, "Hey there, everybody. Stand by, will you?"

The work of replacing the defective section had gone smoothly until the articulated arm of the Robocrane jammed. Theoretically, this could not have happened; and, having happened, the crane was designed to repair itself.

But here again the dilemma of Beaural civilization interposed its special paralysis. A self-repair machine must necessarily have another self-repairing machine behind it to service it; the second must have a third, and the third a fourth, and so on endlessly. Any truly and completely automatic and self-repairing machine must be part of a design, which integrates all the devices in existence: an interdependent, interlocking mechanical civilization. Such a system would be self-sufficient, and humanity would be superfluous; at the end of every path, the bosses of the Plotbureau were faced with this inevitable climax. Since it was one they dared not meet, they temporized as usual, all machines were self-repairing and fully-automatic up to a point; beyond that point, somewhere along the line, there was no automatic, self-repairing machine behind the one which had broken down.   Humanity, in the person of working proles, justified its continued existence.

JO-HANS explained, "It must be jammed in two places. Can't get the boom down where we could work on it.   Lower away," he commanded in demonstration, but the robocrane remained helplessly still, holding its load high in the air.

"What about climbing up and seeing what's jamming the joint?" suggested Will-jim.

"Climb *that?*" jeered Mei-lu, pointing to the limber smoothness, its rippled length stiffened in the glare of the searchlights which brought out all colors of the quonium. "What would you hang on to?"

"Have to send in a call for another crane or a cybrepairer. Which'll it be?"

"Wait," said Fera-liz. "Four arms are better than two; let me try."   Without waiting, she put both pairs of arms around the base of the boom, and endeavored with the aid of her feet to inch her way up.

"No good," judged Will-jim. "You might do all right up where it tapers to a reasonable thickness, but the base is too broad.   I'm afraid Jo is going to have to show off his powers for our new friends."

"Coming at you," said Ed-jo cheerfully, not unmindful of Lil-isa's curious look. "Here goes."

He stepped back two paces, took the slightest of runs, and jumped, soaring into the air. "Oh my," breathed Lil-isa; "oh my."

He landed lightly and easily just behind the top of the crane where it spread out into the three fingerlike ends grasping the load, "Throw some light up here, will you?   I'm all in shadow."

It didn't take more than five minutes to locate the source of one of the troubles—a branch of dead Manzanita which had somehow blown onto the boom and lodged a long, stiff splinter into a thin crack between the crane's articulations. Working it out, he jumped lightly down.

"Something tells me you're going to be useful around here," remarked Jo-hans.

CALLS ON Maintenance Crew Lank 108 were infrequent. There were hours and days when the six had no other obligation but to lounge about the otherwise-empty prole quarters on the eighty fifth floor of the Metro Building, watching the telescreen—or basking under sun lamps. To those of a higher classification this would have represented perfect adjustment; complete leisure spent looking at a telescreen, which automatically strained out excitement from recreation, was the perfect norm.

"Seems pretty silly and wasteful to me," fretted Ed-jo. "The social-adjusters, the Central Troubleshooter, the loyaltycheckers, and all the rest, are supposed to arrange everything so efficiently; yet we spend most of our time in such complete boredom—"

"Where on earth did you pick up that obsolete word?" asked Lil-isa.

"What? Oh, 'boredom'. Jim told me how, in the Dark Ages, when everybody had to be doing something all the time to avoid thinking of the misery of life, they used the word to designate unhappy free time. Of course the Bureau has completely reversed things and the word is, as you say, obsolete; but, being an atavar, I seem to suffer from it. Well, we spend most of our time in such complete boredom that there is really nothing to do but turn on the barbituon and sleep from Firstfeed to Nightfeed. Personally, I'd much rather be out away from the city, out in the wild country; it's far more enjoyable than lying around like an imitation director all day."

"Oooh, what you said," gurgled Mei-lu. "Controversial."

"You couldn't leave the floor, much less the building or the city," Jo-hans pointed out practically. "You couldn't get the password for the day, unless you had proper business."

"The truth is," began Will-jim in that slightly-monotonous voice which indicated the cyclops was marshaling a series of facts in his astonishing memory, "that the world is still vastly overpopulated—in spite of the Happy Despatch, and the rigid denial of reproduction-certificates. Nor is this brought about by the birth of impermissables—who account for only some ten percent of the population. Once there were more than two thousand million people in the world—"

"That's just silly," announced Fera-liz. "There aren't cities enough for them to live in. Or are you going to tell us that the ancients of the Dark Ages had more than twelve cities?"

"As a matter of fact, they did—as you'd know if you'd absorbed any of your history conditioning. But they also lived in the wild country—which wasn't wild in those days, but cultivated. That's another obsolete word, which means that food was grown right on the surface of the land, direct from the soil."

"How quaint," said Mei-lu.

"In the Dark Ages of 1914-2177, the population was reduced by the wars—particularly the so-called Endless War—and their aftermath to a mere handful. I'd say there were less than a hundred thousand wretched and terrified survivors, who realized that men never dare again to use violence if humanity was to escape the extinction that had nearly overtaken it. They built a new civilization, based entirely on efficiency—since war had proved the most inefficient method ever devised for accomplishing anything."

"In the days before the perfection of Informtion—or on Isha or Orsog—you would be a teacher," said Lil-isa, with admiration. For some reason Ed-jo felt annoyed with both her and Will-jim.

WILL-JIM continued, "At first, the most important aims of the Plotbureau—then a small group of surviving scientists, who took their name from one of the two warring governing bodies—were to reconstruct old machines and devise new ones to supply all human wants, and to breed as rapidly as possible to replace the destroyed millions. But the multiplication of machines to serve all man's needs meant that more and more machine-tenders were machines, and the need for human beings to run machines was less and less. The working day of the prole was reduced to six hours, to three, to two hours; and it could have been reduced still further had the Bureau not realized that here, too, they were facing the inevitable conclusion: the uselessness, hence the needlessness of humanity."

"How did they get out of that situation?" asked Ed-jo.

"The Bureau would probably not have been averse to accepting the paradox of an entirely idle race, had not the proles revolted at their idleness and attempted to overthrow the Plotbureau itself," Will-jim said. "At this time, the world's population was more than five hundred million; it was scattered all over the wild country, for the Endless War had made the old cities uninhabitable.

"To guard against further attempts at rebellion, the Bureau immediately set the working day back at six hours so proles would have no time on their hands for discontent. Naturally, this aggravated the problem and reminded archaeologists of the ancient fable of the Dullupyae—a mythical beast who dug holes only to fill them up. The Bureau's solution was to build the twelve cities we know—in every case near the ruins of famous ancient ones—and remove everyone except the gangs, now sent out in rotation to the mines, from all except these twelve cities. All others were concentrated where they would be under constant observation and control.

"They also instituted a long-range program of reducing the population by an earlier and earlier recommendation of the Happy Despatch (originally euthanasia offered only to senile invalids in great pain). They followed this up with review-boards, and the issuance of reproduction-certificates, which throw a stigma on those born without them. In spite of all this, there are still too many people in the world: one hundred and twenty million. The Bureau must find useful work for them to do, or finally resign itself to seeing the human race replaced entirely by machines. Colonization might be a temporary answer—it would be temporary, for conditions on the colonized planets must eventually approximate those of Earth—but Orsog and Isha are not subject to settlement, and Jupiter seems at present unsuitable for colonization on a large scale; the Bureau must remember what happened when Ed-jo was produced there."

"This is dull stuff," yawned Fera-liz. "No wonder I never absorbed much conditioning."

"I don't see why I can't just walk out of the building, password or no," argued Ed-jo, "Who's to stop me if the guards can't use force?"

"Conditioning," answered Lil-isa; "no human being will commit an asocial act."

"What about the women who have impermissible children?" inquired Fera-liz.

"Except that one," amended the dark girl. "The biological drive is so far stronger than propriety."

"Well, I'm a mutant," persisted Ed-jo, "and mutants don't condition well."

"I never listened to such controversial talk in my life," said Mei-lu, "What will you say at your next loyalty-check?"

Ed-jo grunted. Jo-hans said slowly, "Lu has something, you know. Are all mutants so inclined to controversy?"

"Most P7s aren't too well adjusted," stated Will-jim. "The others—the ones who used to be called subnormal—never have a controversial thought."

THE TELESCREEN, which had been lecturing on *Orsogian Eating Habits and Their Effect on Temperamental Differences*, suddenly announced, "Alert Lank Maintenance Crew One-oh-eight. Stoppage in the seawater conveyor. Stand by."

Mei-lu made a face. "Nasty work," she said. "Dank. Clammy."

"Anything is better than nothing," muttered Ed-jo, jumping up, and already picturing Lil-isa clad in a thermo-suit for outdoors, which made her exotic beauty so much more exciting than in its natural, indoor state.

The conveyor ran in a nearly straight line between the ocean and the city, passing at one point perilously near the ruins of Old Lank and its deadly atmosphere. It was of relatively simple design, consisting of a pumping-station, which drew in the salt water and raised it to the basin. Thence it descended by gravity through a series of rotary filters to the vast reservoir beneath the Capitol Building. Bileways—not true bileways, of course, since they ran, not from building to building above the city, but from the reservoir to the basin—gave access to the filtering-stations and brought the byproducts to the city for further processing.

Though the filters were self-cleaning, trouble constantly developed. This time it was at Number 3 Station, close to the ocean. They got out of the jeecars, and Lil-isa paused at the seaward edge of the bileway before following the others into the station. The sun was little more than overhead, and the steady breeze blew her black hair.

"Isn't it wonderful to get away from the buildings, into the free air!"

Ed-jo came over and stood beside her. Away from the sterilized air which circulated through the Metro Building and automatically removed all odors (so that food was practically tasteless—a development thoroughly repugnant to us nowadays, but one quite acceptable and even desirable to the peculiar asceticism of Beaural civilization) he was aware of all the natural redolence around him: the salty sting of brine tinged with the oiliness of drying seaweed, the sweetish scent of vegetation, and—strangest and most disturbing of all—the smell of the girl's hair and body.

She turned to him. "Did you mean what you said, about wanting to get out into the wild country?"

"Sure I did. And nobody was able to tell me why I couldn't.

"It was because we were afraid, Jo."

"What? I don't get you. Who's we? And what were you afraid of?"

"Wait. Let me tell it my way. I think we're probably safe from teletectors here: there's no particular reason why one should be focused on us."

Ed-jo scratched his head. "I don't understand anything. But go on."

"Don't you see: it isn't just the buildings or the city you want to get away from? Both are good and useful things in themselves. Like the machines, which do so much for humanity and would do more if men were not afraid to be made obsolete—as though man were just a flesh-and-blood machine. And like the work, so futile and boresome. The lack of it would drive us to despair and death."

"Say, this was going to be an explanation; instead, you've got me more confused than ever. A thing can't be good and useful if its opposite is good and useful."

"Human work and the work of machines are not opposites, because men can do things that machines—even the most sensitive of Orsogian robots—can't do. Machines can reproduce music and paintings with absolute fidelity, but they can neither compose nor design, except as an extension of an already conceived pattern. They can invent—given specific data of the need to be fulfilled—but they cannot imagine new needs. They can think; they have conditioned reflexes which respond to stimuli, but they cannot speculate on the nature of the universe, or whether time, like space, is curved."

LIL-ISA PUT her hand, slender dark fingers showing up sharply on the neutral plastic stuff of Ed-jo's suit, on his arm. "Don't you see why the dilemma of the Bureau exists, and why the Bureau can never resolve it? In devising a mechanical, efficient system, the Bureau has devised a mechanistic system that rules out all non-material, all spiritual activity? That's why, under the Bureau, man can be superseded; for there is nothing man can do by material means alone which a machine can't do better. But man has a soul as well as a body; free to develop that soul and allow it expression, there can be no reason to limit the perfection of machinery. There is no longer any competition; the two stand finally as complementary to each other.

"Men can and should work six, eight, fourteen hours a day, doing all the things machines can never do, while the machines in turn take care of every want without attention from men. Machines to do what used to be called drudgery—from producing food to making the most extensive mathematical calculations—while men concentrate on pure thought, pure speculation, pure creation. The Bureau can never admit this, for admitting it would automatically mean the Bureau's own abdication. The Boss and the bosses would have to give up their power; classification would cease, for there would be no reason for one man to be a supe or strawb, and another a prole. Review-boards and Happy Despatch would go; so would permission to reproduce, and marital assignments—"

"Oh, come on," exclaimed Ed-jo in shocked tones. "Surely that's going too far. You wouldn't suggest that human beings mate without proper authorization, based on biological data and psychological tests?"

She looked up at him, the slightest twitch at the corners of the red lips in the ebony face. "Does that sound so horrible? Suppose a very intelligent girl had an urge like Fera-liz? Not just a general urge, but a specific one, toward a rather stupid, but lovable man. Don't you think they might be better suited than partners assigned by a series of electronic tubes?"

"It's too confusing," he muttered. She dropped into a more serious tone. "Don't you see: your instinct is perfectly right in wanting to get away from the city. Only it isn't the physical city you want to escape—at least not permanently. You want to get away from the domination of the Plot-bureau; from the ordering and regulating of every moment: from the knowledge that your life-history is a series of holes on a punch-card which will eventually prompt a machine to recommend your premature death."

"You're talking rebellion against the Bureau," said Ed-jo slowly.

Lil-isa gave him a contemptuous look. "Yes, I am. Any review-board being fed a transcription of what I've said would immediately recommend a Happy Despatch. The difference between what I've been saying and the aimless grumbling of you mutants is—"

"Is what?"

"Is that we intend to do something about it."

CHAPTER FOUR

NIELS SVEN-YORN worked in the Metro Building's power plant. He was remarkably old for a prole—nearly forty—and what was still more odd, single; the woman to whom he had been maritally-assigned had received the Happy Despatch years before, and unaccountably he had never gotten a new assignment.

In the vastness of the prole quarters on the eighty-fifth floor, Sven-yorn was conspicuous—and not merely because of his longevity. Often, groups of proles gathered around him and indulged in long conversation. Garrulity among the P7 mutants was accepted as a concomitant of their atavism, and among the extra urban workers as psychological compensation for their occupations; but that normally-employed proles should prefer verbal exchange with one of their kind to watching the telescreen, listening to an audicord, or turning on the barbituon to induce unconsciousness, was inexplicable.

Green Ed-jo's unresponsiveness to the Tradeskill's conditioning had left him a large share of natural curiosity, a faculty definitely not approved by the Plotbureau. His interest in Sven-yorn jumped when he noticed on several occasions that the older man, during the moments when he was not surrounded by other proles, was doing a strange thing. Surreptitiously he was holding a small, compact object in his hands—an object, which seemed to absorb his entire attention, just as a telescreen normally would. The thing appeared to be composed of many layers of some thin material, fastened together at one side. Its usefulness was not apparent, yet Sven-yorn kept staring at it, at intervals lifting a layer by its loose edge and turning it over.

In the days Before Freedom, as everyone knows, the handling of objects, except in the course of work, was practically obsolete. There was little occasion to touch, lift, pull, push or carry anything. The thermal regulation of the buildings at a constant temperature which would seem enervating to us, made the use of clothing functionless, except for those who were compelled to put on thermoplastic suits to go outside.

(We of today, not being under the horrible compulsion to suppress the passions, encourage the wearing of otherwise-superfluous clothing, just as we encourage privacy. This was unthinkable—at least for the proles—under the Bureau, and for the same reasons: to foster the greatest possible intimacy between men and women.)

Food and drink were the inescapable exceptions, but though contact was hardly avoidable, they came from the pneumospensers in such long-handled containers that the fastidiousness of that asensual and asensuous age was appeased, if not served. Trinkets and playthings had long since been discarded. Information which earlier cultures obtained from compasses or watches sliderules and binoculars could still easier be got by saying "Information Please" to the microphoned walls, or going through the slightly more complex speech necessary to set the proper teletectors in motion.

It was not only curiosity then, but something like a sense of prudish shock, which moved Ed-jo at the sight of Sven-yorn fondling the unknown object. Will-jim shook his head when nudged inquiringly. "Why don't you ask Lil-isa? She's been around here longer than we have."

"Afraid she's annoyed with me," confessed Ed-jo. "She talked pretty controversially the day we were out fixing the conveyor and I... Well, I guess I was too astonished at hearing anyone speak of rebellion against the Bureau—"

"Shut up!" ordered Will-jim between his teeth. "Want to get her into trouble? There's probably a teletector on us right now!"

Ed-jo blushed. "It's all right," said Yohsen Jo-hans from behind them. "If there are teletectors taking down what you say, the transcription won't go to the troubleshooter."

"The rebellion against the Bureau then," said Will-jim, "isn't just talk? It's organized?"

"That's right." Jo-hans spoke apologetically toward the cyclops. "I was pretty sure about you, but Lil-isa wanted to sound out our friend here first. When he didn't seem enthusiastic, we thought we'd give him a while to think things over; but spotting Sven-yorn reading a book like this—"

"So that's what he's doing. I've heard about books and reading, but it's supposed to be a lost art."

"All this stuff is over my bead," complained Ed-jo. "First, Jim knows rebellion is organized—"

"Obviously if there is interference between teletectors and the troubleshooter, it is because someone is using the ancient device called sabotage. Now who would sabotage? Who *could* sabotage? Who'd benefit from sabotage? Answer: proles. Not as individuals, but as a conspiratorial group. Hence, organized rebellion. QED."

"What's that mean?"

"Qurious events described."

"Oh. And what's this stuff about books and reading? I thought they were figures of speech."

JO-HANS LED them over to Sven-yorn's cot. "Two members of our crew, Yom," he explained, "who have thought books and reading were figures of speech."

Sven-yorn grinned, showing teeth, which the soft, despised food of those days did nothing to keep strong. "So they are," he said. "So they are today. But figures of speech have an ancestry; before they became abstractions, they existed as concrete realities. For many centuries the written word was the repository of nearly all learning, and the means of conveying nearly all knowledge. Men wrote what they knew—as much as could be conveyed by words—into books; and others read what they had written and then knew nearly as much as their teachers.

"Originally the prime means of human communication had been oral; little by little it was superseded by the visible word, but never entirely replaced. The oral tradition continued to exist, furtively; as a slightly disreputable and disinherited relative; the book, the newspaper, the magazine were dominant. Then, during the early part of the Dark Age, a revulsion occurred: the oral tradition began recapturing lost ground by utilizing the visual process to short-circuit the visual machinery. Pictures were easier to look at than alphabetical symbols, and sounds were easier to hear. The simpler rather than the more complex mental efforts appealed to the human distrust of thought. Reading and writing became lost arts when the need for them vanished, as their place was filled by the television and all its cybernetic allies.

"The Plotbureau, remolding a world from the odds and ends escaping destruction, was satisfied that this should be so. Men who read may get strange and disturbing ideas; those who only hear or see art more docile; they can be more satisfactorily conditioned.

"Reading and writing were never really lost; in every generation there were a few who distrusted the glib openness of the machines, and doggedly kept literacy alive as a safeguard against the failure or treachery of the substitutes. Since books are the only known counteragent to the conditioning which subordinates men to the will of the Bureau, the Readers went to their Happy Despatch early—

but not before they had taught others to read, and so to question the complete benevolence of the twelve bosses and The Boss.

"Long before the Bureau itself perceived it and began to be frightened into passivity; the Readers began to understand the central problem of Beaural civilization. They also realized that the Bureau could never embrace the only possible solution; indeed, they saw that inevitably the Bureau would take courage and destroy mankind by allowing the machines to perfect themselves, without providing at the same time some reason for humanity to continue. Then they knew they would have to free the world from the Bureau."

"Well," said Ed-jo, "That sounds easy enough. There are only thirteen members of the Plot bureau: a few hundred readers could easily take over."

There was a moment of silence. "That almost sounds…" began Mei-lu.

"Don't be ridiculous," said Lil-isa.

"We don't want to 'take over'," explained Sven-yorn gently. "Substituting one set of rulers for another helps nothing; the whole history of the Dark Age is the continuous story of a struggle for power. Furthermore, 'taking over' suggests violence—naturally, you didn't have any such thought in mind—and if there is one luxury humanity can never again afford, it is force."

"In a way," said Lil-isa thoughtfully, "the whole system of conditioning, from juvenry to preversity uses force of a kind. No human refuses a proper order—the Bureau defines 'proper' and then so insistently propounds both the statement and the definition that no human dreams of questioning either. Even when it means accepting death long before it would occur in the natural course."

"But natural death is horrid," exclaimed Fera-liz.

"How do you know? Only because the audicord told you so, over and over—just as it told you how to use Information, or explained the duties of each classification. It repeated it so often that you never think of questioning it, even when it is in direct opposition to all your instincts. The audicord tells you that man spent his whole life in terror of death until the invention of the Happy Despatch—which comes as a glorious and ecstatic experience at exactly the right moment. You believe the audicord, because it has told you at other times that machines exist only for your good— and that machines cannot be constructed to tell you something harmful."

"How do you know that what is written in books is true, while what is spoken through the telescreen is false?" asked Ed-jo stubbornly.

"We don't *know* either of these things. Much that is in books is undoubtedly not true; much that is told us by Information is unquestionably correct. As Readers, we can make a choice between what we believe to be true and what we don't; as passive receivers of conditioning, we have no choice. If man is not free to choose he is not free at all; if he is not free at all, then it is better he become obsolete and be superseded by the machines."

"Teach me to read," said Ed-jo.

ED-JO HAD not conditioned well, nor did he learn to read easily. A certain impatience—not entirely free of contempt—tinged his attitude toward his fellow proles. They were too finicky, too hesitant in coming to grips. If they intended to abolish the Plotbureau why didn't they go ahead and do it, instead of spending so much time talking about it and planning for it?

His impatience was fortified by his increasing realization that the whole structure of society was hollow. The machine appeared to run with utmost smoothness; everything, from permission to reproduce to Happy Despatch went according to plan. Actually, he found, the pattern was a mirage, and had been thus for a long time.

For the Readers had not merely cancelled the intensive conditioning for themselves; they had grasped the illogic at the root of the Plotbureau's dilemma. They found the inadequacies of the machines, and learned how to create new inadequacies. They became, not machine-tenders as had been intended, but technicians, capable of changing the function of the machines—or, if it suited their purpose, making them distort or lie. It was they, not the Bureau, who held the real power.

It was the Readers who had devised the great safety-valve of planetary exploration, to lead the Plotbureau into justifying continued human existence. They used Information and the planning-cybernets to make the bosses think the idea was their own, and set the inventing, blueprinting and construction machines to work on the exmosphliers.

But the Bureau's rigidity eventually balked the push of the Readers, arbitrarily labeling Ishards "primitive" and Orsogians "decadent". This was the excuse for restricting intercourse with them to commence. The Bureau had decreed that Jupiter should be used only for exploiting goochs, even after it was discovered that beneath the unbreathable atmosphere which showed on the spectroscope, there was a mile-high strip of air which would make colonizing simple. Finally the Bureau had declared further exploration of the Solar System pointless, and so sealed the safety-valve the Readers had devised.

None of this new knowledge interested Ed-jo a tenth as much as the discovery that his notion of escaping from the city to the wild country was not so fantastic as he'd thought.

In remote spots, communities of Readers existed—unknown to the Bureau or the perpetual census.

"'Readers who were prescribed a Happy Despatch and their descendents,'" he repeated. "I suppose they were smuggled out of the euthanoriums; why aren't non-Readers smuggled out, too?"

"Because non-Readers haven't neutralized their conditioning," explained Lil-isa; "when they're offered escape from the Happy Despatch, they're horrified. They're not only convinced they are going to perfect bliss, but that to evade the decision of a review-board—a machine devised solely for human benefit—would be barbarous."

"By this time there must be a lot of them—wild Readers, I mean."

"There are a lot of free Readers. Since they have no marital-assignments, or reproduction-certificates, their number increases fast. It won't be many years till there are as many people in the communities as the cities. It isn't only the increased birthrate, but natural death at fifty to a hundred, instead of the Happy Despatch at twenty-five or thirty."

"But how do they live? How do they get food, for instance, without hydroponic tanks?"

"They have hydroponic tanks smaller than those in the buildings, but pretty much the same. They aren't dependent on them though, as we proles are, but enjoy a varied diet— even more varied than those of the upper classifications."

"I don't see what difference it makes," said Ed-jo indifferently. "Food is food. You have to eat to keep alive, and what you eat has to contain the elements necessary to nutrition; beyond that, what does it matter whether it's varied or not?"

LIL-ISA TOSSED her head. "What difference does it make who your marital assignment is? Men are men and women are women; all they need is the necessary vitamins, or genes, or something."

"That's right; what are you looking so mad about?"

"Nothing you could possibly understand. Let's see— where were we?"

"Varied diet."

"Yes. They farm the land, growing food directly in the soil."

"Sounds unsanitary," remarked Ed-jo dubiously.

"They have also learned the ancient art of domesticating animals, so that herds of tamed bison and antelope provide milk and meat. They have small factories for the making of synthetic materials, but they also use many natural ones. They could produce power themselves, but they find it more convenient to tune in on the power-plants of the cities nearest them."

"Doesn't that show up on the tabulators?"

"There are Readers in every assignment, more all the time. Simple adjustments keep the tabulators registering only normal consumption."

"I don't see, with all this activity going on, how they manage to keep their existence secret."

"That's because you don't yet realize how completely isolated the higher classifications are. They depend on Information, and the perpetual census, and other cybernets— which, in turn, are dependent upon such machines as teletectors using radar and sonar. The communities have anti-sonar devices which generally baffle the teletectors; if they fail, the Readers in the cities suppress the data before it gets to the Bureau. Also the inertia of the bosses is profound. Rebellion; Readers; escape from the Happy Despatch; communities in the wild country—none of these are provided for in the scheme of Beaural civilization. Therefore, no one looks for such things—or would believe the rumor of them, unless confronted with the actual fact. Which the Readers take good care they aren't."

"So I suppose the Readers inside will just wait for the time when the communities have grown bigger than the cities to join them and leave the buildings to decay?"

"Why should you suppose that? The cities and the civilization, such as it is, don't belong to the Bureau; they are everyone's inheritance. Not only has history taught us the danger of dividing the world, but if life is valuable—and Readers certainly believe it is—then it wouldn't be right to leave behind us proles and even higher classifications (who might become Readers), for assignment and Happy Despatch instead of a full existence. A new civilization of Readers can't exist side-by-side with the old civilization of the Bureau."

"But when I said the Readers could take over very easily, everybody jumped on me."

"'It was silly of us, wasn't it? But you know, to an over-sensitive ear, it almost sounded as though you meant using force. This is not a struggle for power, such as they used to have in the Dark Age. We won't 'take over'; the Bureau will abdicate."

He laughed. "I can just imagine The Boss and the bosses abdicating. Or are the Readers planning to jam the cybernets so that they will recommend a Happy Despatch for all the higher classifications?"

Her look was puzzled, distressed, angry. "I know you don't mean what you seem to mean, but that odd, atavistic way of talking does give the false impression that you aren't normally horrified of all forms of violence."

Ed-jo shrugged his shoulders. "Jim says there's an ancient proverb: 'All's fair in war...' and something else. Something obsolete. I forget just what," he muttered.

CHAPTER FIVE

FOR SOME days, the maintenance crew had not been called out. Green Ed-jo oscillated between fits of dogged determination, during which he persisted steadily in his attempt to master the art of reading, and moods, which made him throw the primer aside. He lay on his cot now, looking at neither book nor telescreen.

"Jim!"

"Huh?" The cyclops was deeply absorbed and did not lift his eye from the page.

"Listen: don't you ever wonder if, after all, the Readers are entirely right and the Bureau entirely wrong?"

Will-jim put down his book. "Mean you've suddenly realized utopia won't necessarily materialize fifteen minutes after the Bureau abdicates?"

"For one thing I don't believe the Bureau *will* abdicate. Why should it? Without the bosses and The Boss, without the experience and training of the upper classifications, the proles are helpless. We have no leaders, and the Readers make it a matter of principle to deny the necessity of leadership."

"And you have come to the conclusion that men have to be led for their own good?"

"Hadn't thought of it in those words exactly. I was only realizing that people—especially proles—need direction; otherwise nothing would ever get done. But the way you say it sounds better, maybe. 'For their own good.' Yes. Yes, I do."

Ed-jo paused for a moment, then went on. "I don't know what 'utopia' means, exactly—one of your obsolete words. What I was getting at was something like this: certainly the rule of the Bure means no good for the future of mankind—but what do the Readers intend to substitute for it? Nothing."

"'Nothing' is a big word," said Will-jim thoughtfully, "and I don't think it is exact in this case. So far as the Bureau is anything at all but a useless survival, a museum-piece, a dead weight, the Readers will substitute the human spirit, curiosity, adventurousness, enthusiasm. To substitute nothing for something would be a negative advance; but on the contrary, the Readers propose something for nothing. For the Bureau is nothing, and the routine to which it subjects humanity is mere senseless going through the motion."

"I can't argue with you when you begin talking like that," answered Ed-jo sulkily. "All I know is that without some kind of leadership, nothing will ever get done—"

"What needs to be done so badly that man has to give up his freedom to accomplish it? Only the Bureau blocks the perfection of the machines which could fill all material needs. As for the non-material ones, the Bureau is unaware of their existence; what leadership is required to produce books, paintings, music or new wants?"

Ed-jo continued obstinately as though he had not been interrupted. "All I know is that, without some kind of order, it wouldn't be long before the earth is overrun by Ishards and Orsogians."

"Ah..." Will-jim looked at him contemplatively. "The prospect of extraterrestrial immigration disturbed you?"

"Well, shouldn't it?"

"I think you ought to have a long talk with Isa about it."

ED-JO, LIKE a man who has had an unpleasant shock which he still partially disbelieves, looked sullenly at the ground. "I do think someone might have told me these things. Evidently everyone else but me has been let in on the facts."

The aqueduct had suffered a leak far from Lank, many miles to the north, in a wild country quite unlike the wild country he had learned to know. Giant trees grew all around, grew straight up into a thick fog. Their discarded needles, brown, yellowish or gray, padded the earth with a soft, springy cover through which narrow streams of water ran, and lush weeds forced rank leaves. Both Ed-jo and Lil-isa were dressed in lignyon parkas to keep out the cold.

"I don't think you understand." Lil-isa's beautiful, dark face was expressive in the dull air. "One learns as fast as one wishes—no faster. Jim's logic and grasp of history made him wonder why the Bureau was so frightened of the infiltration of inhabitants from other planets. The excuse that we of Isha are backward and primitive, and the people of Orsog decadent, didn't seem to make sense."

"But it does," burst out Ed-jo. "If you are really an Ishard—and I suppose I have to take your word for it, because no one's going to admit themselves humanoid if they aren't—you must be different from other Ishards. I'd never have known if you hadn't told me. And it certainly is a well-known fact the Orsogians are decadent—an old, worn-out, senile race. Individual exceptions don't alter the desirability of keeping these humanoids away from contaminating contact with mankind."

Lil-isa's eyes for the first time seemed alien and perhaps for that reason more beautiful than before. She spoke in a dispassionate voice, which did not entirely hide her anger. "Isha's recent origin as an inhabitable planet, far from supporting the Bureau's propaganda that we must necessarily be a primitive species, merely indicates that insufficient time has passed for life of any kind to have developed on Isha."

"If life never developed on Isha then you don't exist. You're something I dreamed up," said Ed-jo with a triumphant laugh.

"There are other ways of life coming to a world besides developing there indigenously, as you yourself ought to know. You come from Jupiter, yet your ancestors didn't evolve from goochs."

"I should say not. My parents were organizers, sent there from earth."

"Exactly; and my ancestors also came from earth. Not as organizers for a thorough exploitation and robbery, or to remake the colonial planet into an image of the mother one with all its faults, but as emigrants, sick of the wars and oppression which seemed inevitable on this globe. In the days of the Emperor Fu-hi, long before the Second Dark Age which your history conditioners ignorantly call *the* Dark Age, long before the civilization of Rome or Greece or Egypt—"

"Jim was telling me something about them," muttered Ed-jo. "A bunch of savages. No machines."

"—there was a highly-advanced culture in the world, occupying a small portion of the globe. These civilized people called themselves the sons of Han. They were surrounded by barbarians who conquered them at intervals, were absorbed into their culture, only to face new assaults from the outside. Despairing—perhaps too soon—of mankind, my ancestors (many of whose minor inventions like gunpowder, paper-making, printing and so forth, later trickling to the occident, were hailed as colossal strides in the march of progress) built a great number of space ships—"

"Exmosphliers!"

"No. They operated on entirely different principles. Revisiting the earth from time to time to recheck their pessimistic appraisal, they were mistaken generally for natural phenomena—though during the early part of the Second

48

Dark Age they were recognized as vehicles. Into these space ships the sons of Han packed not only those humans willing to undertake the adventure, but seeds of all useful trees and plants known to them; the spawn of fish and pairs of sea animals; beneficent insects; and beasts and fowl. Since they were versed in astronomy they chose Isha as their destination, rather than Orsog—which they believed, quite correctly, to be already inhabited.

"ON ISHA—they got the name from a still older people—they built, literally, a new world, free at last from the threat of barbarism and released from the burden of war. Possibly because of the inexhaustible richness of the Ishard soil, possibly for philosophic reasons, we did not develop a mechanical civilization; or rather we did not build a civilization dependent upon machines, though we have always produced individuals who enjoyed tinkering with gadgets, and constructing new marvels for pleasure and astonishment.

"Perhaps the only disturbing factor in our world was the thought of the planet left behind. We could not, nor did we want to, shake off all responsibility, for those who were, after all, of our blood. From time to time our ancient space-ships visited the earth for observation, only to return with the same grim story: man was incapable as ever of achieving his destiny. There was nothing we could do to help. When the succession of self-made catastrophes which characterized the Second Dark Age culminated in the last orgy of destruction, and reduced the population of the earth to a bare handful, and the survivors sincerely forswore force forever, we had great hopes—only to see them sink as the domination of the Bureau was accepted instead of freedom.

"Hope brightened again when we learned that some proles retained and transmitted the art of reading. We welcomed the first exmosphliers, but the higher classifications who composed the authority on board had no interest in us but a commercial one. Because we worked with our hands, and had long since given up building great cities, they catalogued us as backward and primitive humanoids. It was only when contact was made with proles who turned out to be Readers, that the Ishards saw that our function could be to encourage them and help them change the earth. As a consequence, Readers who were supposed to have had the Happy Despatch came to Isha and not only taught boys and girls all they knew, but rehearsed selected volunteers so exhaustively that we were able to take our places in the buildings as proles without the slightest suspicion."

"Ah," exclaimed Ed-jo.

"Of course Readers fixed the perpetual census, the adjusters, and the troubleshooter so that we were accounted for properly."

"But why?" demanded Ed-jo. "Why couldn't you leave the people of earth to solve their own problems without outside interference?"

"Oh, Jo, Jo—how can you be so thoroughly conditioned? There is collective responsibility and collective guilt in the body of an individual, in the world, in the universe. If something went wrong with your leg, you wouldn't think of letting it solve its own problems without outside interference from your arms."

Lil-isa paused before going on. "It was through the Readers on board the exmosphliers that we made our first contact with the people of Orsog. Our space ships were capable only of the distance from Isha to earth and return, or one way to Orsog. In spite of this, several expeditions had set out for the red planet, after which nothing was heard of them. We now learned that they had landed safely and been welcomed, but the Orsogians made no attempt to help them return or communicate with us. Orsogian civilization is mechanical, like Earth's, but the Orsogian's long ago eschewed space travel or active communication with other worlds. Our people didn't discover the elements used for refueling on Orsog: it's possible they don't exist there. The Ishards made the best of it, intermarried with the Orsogians. Their descendants are indistinguishable from other inhabitants of the planet, the dark color our skins acquired on Isha bleaching out in a few generations to the paleness characteristic of Orsog."

"And Jim figured all this out for himself?" asked Ed-jo skeptically.

"Of course not. But he made the initial step of questioning the exclusive attitude of the Bureau: from that to deducing that there might be Ishards or Orsogians among the Readers was a short step. Questions brought out the whole story because Jim was ready to learn."

"You don't think I'm ready to learn. Why have you told me all this?"

Lil-isa smiled tenderly at him. "Does it matter why? I could say reasonably enough that we could not afford to let you remain ignorant. Or that your acceptance of the Bureau's viewpoint about Ishards or Orsogians was hurtful. Or that the Readers have discovered what we Ishards have always known: that all spirit is equally valuable, and no man is to be despised, left behind, sacrificed, used, or deemed inferior. But I would rather say that we Ishards have not been conditioned to suppress or be ashamed of our emotions…"

He looked distrustfully at the lovely dark face. She reached out a tentative hand, then let it drop to her side when he made no attempt to respond.

CHAPTER SIX

THE DAMAGE to the aqueduct at this point was not accidental. The concentration of free Readers in this vicinity was large, and their need for water was great. They could have dug wells, dammed the river from above the aqueduct to Lank. Conceiving the fruits of civilization to be common property, they saw no reason to do any of these things; it was much easier to hook on to the big pipeline.

They could have fabricated pipe and joined it to the aqueduct. They had machines, and machines to make machines, but their technology had not yet caught up with the cities', nor was there any point in forcing its progress feverishly. There were too many other aspects of civilization, neglected by the Plotbureau, to work on.

So the cybernets had obligingly been tampered with, requisitions put through, and the finished pipe shipped by freightcopter. Again, the free Readers could have put the pipe together by primitive methods; instead the maintenance crew came to do the job.

"And what will happen when it appears we took a week on a job that should have been finished in a few hours?" asked Ed-jo.

"Nothing," replied Jo-hans. "Because it won't appear; the records will be fixed."

"Everything's coming to depend more and more on cooked records and gummed-up machinery. Suppose we're called on in a real emergency meanwhile?"

"Cooked records again," answered Will-jim. "Morally (remind me to explain this archaic word) indefensible. Another reason for confronting the Bureau with the facts and demanding their abdication as soon as possible."

Fera-liz said abruptly, "Isn't Billyum the most gorgeous hunk of man?"

"Who's Billyum?" asked Lil-isa.

"One of the wild Readers," said Fera-liz. "You missed him when you were out looking into Jo's eyes."

"Where did you pick up this vocabulary, Liz?" inquired Will-jim.

Fera-liz waved four arms lightly. "Boy, I'm hep now; these wild jakes know their scallions."

THE ADJECTIVE "wild" became more understandable as they became better acquainted with Billyum and his companions. The free Readers had an air of assurance, vitality and energy that even the most vigorous urban Readers lacked. They showed a zest, which made the cities appear abodes of the dead, in contrast.

For miles around, the wild country had been tamed. Except for forest bands crossing the open ground at intervals, the brush had been cleared and crops were growing: bright green corn, dull green wheat, lush green alfalfa. In the midst of the farmland was the Readers' town.

Although work on the new branch of the aqueduct went on, night and day, the maintenance crew spent much of their time in this town. By Beaural standards, as by ours of today, it was cruel. The buildings—they were only three—were less than forty stories high, and their whole area was less than that of the base of the Metro Building at Lank—even though parks, many times wider than the gardens of the metropolis, were laid out between them.

There were no guards, no passwords, no assignments. "I don't understand," said Mei-lu: "without all the machinery of Lank there's more work to be done. How can it be done without order?"

"But we have order," explained Billyum. "We know what there is to do and we do it. Each of us, whether born free or escaped from a Happy Despatch, chooses an occupation to his liking—"

"At what age?" asked Will-jim.

"At any age. Soon as he or she wants to do anything."

"Children?"

"Why not? The ancients rejected child labor because the children were forced to work. With us, a child can choose an occupation and work or play at it. If anything is accomplished, good; if not, nothing is lost."

"Suppose an adult, having chosen an occupation, wants to change?"

"Why then he changes, naturally."

"How often?"

"As often as he likes. Would you expect us to force him to do something distasteful?"

"But suppose he decides not to work at all?"

"That's happened—but never for long. We have no barbituons here to relieve boredom. But even if someone refused to do his share, why should we refuse to feed him, or stigmatize him? But it has never happened."

"Isn't this parceling out of jobs very haphazard?"

"No more than the selection by machines fumbling with holes in punch-cards. Certainly, if the incidence of Happy Despatches mean anything, it is better suited to humanity."

The food in Sonom—as the Readers' town was called, after an ancient settlement believed to have been located in the vicinity—was strange to the maintenance crew. They were first repelled and then filled with strange feelings of guilt, so that they glanced apprehensively at each other between mouthfuls.

To a great extent what they ate was identifiable to them, but this superficial familiarity only made its foreignness more disturbing. The fruit and vegetables had, except to the deepest scrutiny, the appearance of their hydroponic counterparts; but they also had distinct and individual smells, a different consistency and an almost acrid effect on the taste buds.

It was the proteins, however, which struck them as being at once offensive and shamefully attractive. The rich, lusty aroma; the close knit texture requiring the aid of a sharp cutting edge to sever it into edible pieces; the strong, redolent juices oozing out when the cuts were made, were totally unlike the nutritious wafers of dehydrated gouch or synthetic lactin served in the cities at Nightfeed.

"It's animal," exclaimed Mei-lu suddenly.

"Of course it is," said Billyum. "Buffalo. We've domesticated some of the herd."

"I didn't mean that. I meant the eating of it is animal. Chew, chew, chew; gnaw, gnaw, gnaw; then gulp. As in the ancient books, or history-conditioning."

"We are animals," said Will-jim placidly. "That's what the Bureau has forgotten. Like animals, our instinct is to be free."

NIGHTFEED was very unlike Nightfeed at Lank. Unquestionably partaking of something of the same quality of communal ritual, it was more leisurely, noisier, and obviously enjoyable rather than solemn. Many of the Readers ate in small, sociable groups, or by themselves, with an open book propped in front of them—a procedure unthinkable in the cities where all partook of food with eyes fixed on the telescreen.

Most eccentric to Ed-jo were the dormitory arrangements. The whole concept of privacy, so cherished by the ancient Anglo-Saxons, had come under stronger and stronger attack during the Dark Ages until it was regarded as a repulsive atavism. No greater bar to uniformity of thinking—and consequently unanimity of obedience to proper orders—could be conceived than temporary or permanent withdrawal from the sight and sound of others. This was why the prole quarters in the buildings were vast sweeps of empty floors, broken only by the couches set with mathematical regularity and evenness, and the telescreens above, with their vocally-operated controls, set flush like the servadors beside them.

The difference in the accommodations of the Readers, even allowing for their more primitive technology and facilities, was startling. Maritally-assigned men and women (Ed-jo's prudery was still shocked at the thought of voluntary and haphazard marriage; he tried to think of the arrangements decently, as assignments) had walled-off cubicles with doors, to which they retired at night, or whenever the notion struck them. Even their children, indelicately associated with parents long after they should have been in a juvenry, joined in this immodest privacy.

Billyum inquired if any of the three couples desired such a cubicle. Fera-liz giggled and wanted to know if Billyum would share it with her; both Lil-isa and Ed-jo hesitated a perceptible fraction of time before shaking their heads.

For the first time since they had played as children in the Lank Tradeskill Ed-jo hid his thoughts from Will-jim and Fera-liz. Nor did he any longer ask Lil-isa, Jo-hans or Sven-yorn the first questions that came into his head. Now he calculated his speech for the effect it would have on others.

For Green Ed-jo had found a viewpoint which was both positive and his own. The spectacle of the embryonic Readers' society convinced him that their philosophy was basically wrong. While there was no doubt in his mind that the rule of the Bureau was inefficient and deleterious, at the same time it seemed to him that neither the method nor the goals of the Readers was calculated to achieve an over-whelming improvement.

The Readers were right in wishing to solve the Plotbureau's dilemma by freeing men from all work which could be done by machines; as for the substitution of creative, or speculative, activity Green Ed-jo was dubious, being unable to conceive exactly what forms such activity would take. He thought it would undoubtedly be more prac-tical for mankind, released from drudgery, to go adventuring and colonizing—really colonizing, this time through the solar system as once they had over the face of the earth. But for this, or for any other way of life that Ed-jo could visualize as desirable, order was needed. And in spite of Billyum's arguments and his companions' concurrence, order to Ed-jo meant centralized planning, and leadership. Both were needed too for the job of replacing the Bureau, for it seemed to him ridiculous to think, as the Readers did, that the bosses would just gracefully yield their power.

Power was the key. You could misuse power as the Bureau undoubtedly did, or not use it at all as the Readers proposed. But misused or unused, power existed. It could be used for good. In ancient times men had arisen with burning visions of an ordered world. The history books and the telecorders' conditioning were agreed in calling them bad and evil men. Perhaps they were, but the idea of leadership and order were not bad or evil. Power itself was neither good nor bad; only the way it was used. If, when the Readers bumbled and muddled and failed, and a leader arose to straighten out the affairs of mankind with a strong and sure hand—

It was conceivable that that leader could be someone like Green Ed-jo.

It was conceivable the leader could *be* Green Ed-jo.

BIT BY BIT the pretense of subservience to the Bureau crumbled. Readers from the outside came and went in Lank at will. These were the very individuals who had been recommended a Happy Despatch and who supposedly, after a week of wild debauch with instruments of dissipation which had not known any other use for generations, had been reduced to dust and blown into the atmosphere along with other dried and powdered waste. Conditioned proles were frequently startled to see evidence of the forgotten theological doctrine of resurrection.

This same increasing carelessness applied to tampering with the machines: records of power-consumption were not always adjusted precisely to account for diversion to the Readers' communities; projects were embarked upon without previously faking assignments. The Readers behaved as though they were daring the Bureau to discover their doings.

Sven-yorn admitted as much. "We want the bosses to learn gradually that their dominance is illusory and that the machines which govern mankind are not only fallible but subject to us whenever we wish them so. For if they were to find out the true state of affairs all at once, the shock might stiffen their resistance and cause unhappy complications. By allowing suspicion to develop into knowledge we make it easier for them to take the next step—resignation."

"But by giving them warning, you allow them time to prepare to resist the change," argued Ed-jo.

"What can they do?" asked Sven-yorn. "Issue orders? The Readers will not obey them, for they have neutralized their conditioning. The proles still conditioned to obey will never hear them, for Readers will block their transmission. The same thing applies to reassignments, or review-boards which would recommend Happy Despatches. No, no; the only preparation the bosses can make is to become proles."

"Just sort of drift into a new society?"

"Not exactly. We have already tampered with the preversty conditioning; our next step is to see to the issuance of unlimited permits to reproduce. Then comes the change in the system of marital assignments—"

"Wow!" exclaimed Fera-liz.

"Funny thing's been happening lately," commented Johans. "There seems to have been an inexplicable increase in food-consumption among the higher classifications."

"Maybe they've taught their robots to eat," giggled Mei-lu.

WHEN THE inexplicable was explained, the Readers found no amusement in it. One morning, during Firstfeed, there appeared on all the telescreens the presentation of a bulky figure reclining on a couch.

"This is Smid Jor-al, Boss of Lank, The Boss. I am speaking to all the people of the earth. I advise you, insubordinate so-called Readers, not to interfere with this broadcast. This advice is for your own good, because any interference will automatically result in disaster—as you will soon see.

"You are misled, and are misleading yourselves. You would abolish the Plotbureau, level all classifications, do away with assignments, end the Happy Despatch. You think that that way lies freedom. You are wrong; that way lies overpopulation, anarchy, and a return to the miseries and wretchedness our ancestors suffered. Believe me, you cannot tamper with the structure of civilization—and the Bureau represents the only real, thorough and secure civilization man has ever known—without bringing the whole building down on you.

"However, I know this isn't the moment for argument or reason. My time is short and some foolish individual may make it even shorter at any moment by disconnecting me. I will therefore stick to facts. In a few minutes, all the power will go off and the world will be helpless and stagnant; since your parasitical communities of Readers are also dependent on the power generated in the cities they will be unable to come to your assistance.

"We of the Plotbureau are quite aware that you are capable of restoring the power; we are not as foolish as you seem to think. Yes, you could turn the power back on seconds after I shut it off. Incidentally it is now adjusted to go off negatively; that is, I don't have to give an affirmative command, but merely to stop talking. An interval of silence will work the relays. That is one of the reasons it would be unwise to cut me off before I've finished.

"But when the power is off do not, I beg you, be so foolish as to restore it except by our consent. For when the power goes back on—unless the correct password is fed to the master-controls on Information—that invaluable cybernet will destroy itself. It has been so adjusted.

"I need hardly point out, even to the unintegrated, what a calamity the destruction of Information would be. All the accumulated knowledge of mankind would vanish instantly. Even if it were possible to reconstruct it out of those books in which you take such pride—and it is not, for so many books have been lost, and so much knowledge has been achieved since Information was built—it would take years, if not generations. You could not hope to continue as anything more than primitive anthropoids without Information.

"We of the upper classifications have been storing food for a long time against this day. We shall only suffer inconvenience while the power is off ; you, however, will be helpless.

"When you are ready to give up your insubordination we will let you have the word to use on the controls of Information. Some of you may argue that it would be clever to deceive us—to pretend submission and then repudiate your surrender when Information functioned again. We have anticipated this by providing for follow-up passwords at various time-intervals, without which destruction will then take place. Your only choice is to give in—sincerely.

"Since the shutting off of power will cut communications between us, you will have to find another means of letting us know your submission beside the telescreen, elevator, or helicopter. How you will get together to decide among yourselves of the inevitability of capitulation I have no idea, since the elevators won't run nor the electronic doors open with the power shut off. As for communication between the cities, that is obviously out of the question. So it will remain with you of Lank to submit for all of you; during the daylight hours, one of us will be at a window facing the aerial gardens on the same side as the main entrance to the Beaural Building. Perhaps the Readers who are so ready to run the world will find a way to get out there from the books they value so highly. They may also find the answer to the food problem, which doubtless will become pressing in a day or so—except for those few now in the same room with hydroponic tanks or meal-processors.

"But I digress, for the subject has been pleasant. Assuming that you get together, or that your leaders are on ground level (and able in some way to get through the entrance doors) you will rig up some kind of white flag—this will appeal to your archaeological enthusiasms, your taste for antique—so we can see it. We will then transmit to you the password. It will require a little ingenuity to figure out, and you will not be absolutely sure of the correctness of your interpretation until you have staked everything on it—but this is the penalty for dedicating yourselves to the good of mankind instead of filling the duties of your assignments. The power will now go off."

The sardonically-smiling face of Smid Jor-al remained on the telescreens for ten seconds. Then they went blank.

At the same moment, the lights went off.

CHAPTER SEVEN

THE CONFUSION of voices, rising and falling in the dusky gloom, which appeared darker than it was because of its suddenness and strangeness, finally resolved itself into two elements. The loudest and sharpest came from proles in panic, hysterically demanding that something be done right away; berating the Readers for their senseless sedition; crying that the air-conditioning was off, and they would suffocate; complaining that they could not see.

The calmer voices, rising now and then in exasperation, were those of the Readers, urging quiet, shouting that there was nothing to fear that even though the conditioning was off air was still entering from the vents. As for seeing, as soon as eyes became accustomed, the light coming through the windows—though dim, except within fifty meters or so— was nevertheless strong enough even in the center to allow them to make out and recognize objects and people. There was no cause for panic; everything would be taken care of.

"Will it?" muttered Green Ed-jo; "I wonder."

In spite of the reassurances of the Readers there was a heavy, stunning sense of helplessness in the air. Conditioning had established the image of the Plot bureau as a benevolent overseer, existing only to further the wellbeing of mankind, without whose wise and experienced direction civilization would collapse. Now, suddenly this paternal figure showed itself in wrath, withdrawing its support and comfort from its dependents, leaving them in dark, terrified anxiety. Even the

Readers, quite apart from their position of responsibility, knew the quaking feeling of uneasiness.

"If I'd had any sense I'd have ordered a thermo-suit while Smid was speaking," came Fera-liz' voice. "I'm getting goose-pimples from the cold."

"Imagination," said Will-jim; "the temperature couldn't have fallen half a degree yet."

In the gloom Ed-jo saw Lil-isa close beside him. Almost without volition he reached toward her. Each leaned; their lips touched. It was an unfamiliar gesture; kissing was not customary in Beaural civilization.

It was Ed-jo who pulled away first. "Now that the Readers have lost out," he said harshly, "one of the first things the Bureau will probably do is search out all you Ishards and send you back where you came from."

"What makes you think the Readers have lost?" she asked calmly.

"What makes you doubt it?" he retorted, "What else are they to do but give in? With their altruism, and concern for the welfare of all humanity, they certainly won't allow Information to be destroyed. Nor will they let the proles starve while they try to figure out some way to improve their position."

"Don't be so pessimistic," put in Jo-hans. "I bet right now the Readers in the powerhouse are planning how to get things going again."

"That's the trouble with the whole setup. Everybody depending on everybody else; no direction, no leader at the top, no secrets; everything wide open and vulnerable."

"And how would you manage if you were the leader you think so essential?" inquired Sven-yorn.

"Why, I would have—"

"Would-haves are no use now. What would you do from here on?"

"Well," began Ed-jo, "I'd turn the tables on the upper classifications. Starve them out."

"They may have food and water for a week, a month, or a year. Whatever period it is, the proles would be starved out first."

ED-JO ALMOST argued, "Sometimes you have to sacrifice a part for the good of the whole; let the weaker proles succumb, and the stronger survive to rule the world." But he held the words back. The Readers, with their sentimentality, would not agree with this sensible approach. Instead he said, "The proles needn't starve; it's a simple matter of transporting the food from the hydroponic tanks, or the processors, to them—or better, them to the food. As for water, it is right here in the pipes; since the outlets don't work on word of command with the power shut off, we'll just break off the outlets and substitute some kind of plug."

"I'm afraid you don't see the difficulties," contended Will-jim. "No doubt, Readers down below with access to metal are already constructing makeshift hand tools on the ancient model. In time, they could make some kind of ladders or stairways that would reach us up here on the eighty-fifth floor and higher. But it couldn't be done in an hour or a day— maybe not even in a week. By that time we would have lost great numbers from sickness spread by the sewage, no longer carried off, since the flushing mechanism requires power to operate at verbal command. As for the simple device of breaking off the water outlets, you forget that none of the water used in Lank comes to us by force of gravity; many power-pumps lift it. Even if these things could be solved here, what of the eleven other cities? Are we to try and save ourselves while letting their proles die?"

"You intend to surrender, then?"

"No, we intend to think, to reason," said Sven-yorn. "We have time for that, even though we haven't time for wild adventures."

"There's a time for thought, and a time for action," muttered Ed-jo.

"Exactly. Thought comes first; action later. We have several advantages, which the Bureau doesn't. We have choice, which the Bureau deprived itself of when it turned off the power. The gamble is theirs, not ours: they have everything to lose; we can, at worst, only gain less than our full object. They can do nothing now but wait for our decision; we have many alternatives, even after surrender is ruled out. We can, I hope, figure out some way to circumvent the Bureau's move. Or we can turn on the power and allow Information to destroy itself. Terrible as the loss would be, it would not be as bad as The Boss stated; it would not be irreparable for generations. We could continue without it, though the Bureau could not. Or we could attempt to bargain."

"Bargain I What have you to offer them?"

"Let me go on listing some of our advantages first. We alone can restore the power now; it can no longer be done verbally. Even if the Bureau were able to reach the machines from the five-hundredth floor, unless the power is already on nothing changes the audible pattern into a mechanical one. If we are faced by an ultimatum from the Bureau, the Bureau is faced by helplessness without us.

"Then we can, thanks to literacy, communicate among ourselves, at least so far as the Readers in Lank are concerned. The Bureau is limited to those within sound of each others' voices. We have access a great body of knowledge in books; the Bureau has only the odds and ends in its collective memory, without Information. Perhaps most important of all, we have definite objectives in mind; the

Bureau's sole purpose is to attempt restoration of conditions, not as they were, but as its members imagine they used to be. Everything is on our side."

"I'm cold," announced Mei-lu. "If everything is on our side please get me a thermo-suit right away."

THERE WAS no question now that the temperature had fallen. Nor was this due solely to the absence of air-conditioning, for Readers close to the windows had succeeded in making holes in the plexiglas in order to see out.

"Time is passing; the few hours we have are being used up and you do nothing but talk," burst out Ed-jo. "Action; I want to see some action!"

Someone at a window shouted, "They're doing something down below. Can't make out what it is—too far."

"See," said Sven-yorn; "action and calculation at the same time. Now back to considering the situation: The Boss promised a password to protect Information when we got the power on, providing we surrendered. This must mean the Bureau has devised some means of communicating with us from the five hundredth floor. Now they cannot come down to us, nor can we reach them, since neither the elevators nor the copters will run. It is unlikely any of the upper classifications have learned to read and write, just to communicate a single word—so unlikely that I think we can rule it out."

He paused, then went on. "I have read that in ancient times messages were sent from one part of a building to another by tapping on pipes or walls. It is hardly probable the bosses have this bit of information; but even if they did, or figured it out for themselves, it would still leave the problem of our understanding their message—a code held in common, which we don't possess. I think we can rule that out as well."

From the window a prole said, "I still can't make out what they're doing; but whatever it is, others at the windows on the first few floors are in on it."

Sven-yorn continued, "The apparent plan would seem to be to throw some easily-identifiable object from the window. The name of the object would be the password."

"That's logical," agreed Jo-hans.

"All right. An object—not too small, lest it be lost in falling nearly a mile. This pretty well excludes anything which could have been delivered through a servador and kept in readiness."

"But not something which could have been taken up in an elevator or brought down from the roof ahead of time," objected Lil-isa.

"Right." Sven-yorn was silent for a moment. "I hadn't thought of that. Truth is, I had a pet theory and was trying to fit everything into it. I was sure they would throw a robot from the window and that 'Robot' was bound to be the key word. Now... Well, it could be almost anything."

"Look here," interrupted Ed-jo, "I'm sick of all this chatter that gets us nowhere. Let me go and talk to the Bureau face-to-face."

"There's only two things wrong with that," commented Sven-yorn; "the first is, you can't get there; the second is you have nothing to say to the bosses."

"You're half wrong anyway," corrected Mei-lu. "Jo can reach the five hundredth floor easily enough."

"I don't know how easy it would be, but I think I could do it. Anyway, I'd like to try."

WILL-JIM explained Ed-jo's peculiarity, adding, "Why can't he point out that the Bureau has overreached itself by shutting off the power? That since they are dedicated to efficiency and profitable activity, this move of theirs thwarts their own purposes. They no longer direct the world; in actuality the Readers have been doing this for some time; they would be better off to accept the fact and work with us instead of against us."

Fera-liz murmured to no one in particular, "If they weren't so mean about marital-assignments, I'm sure everything would be all right and everybody would be happy."

"I don't suppose any of the bosses know about Jo," reflected Lil-isa. "In ordinary circumstances (if you can imagine ordinary circumstances in which a prole would come in contact with the Bureau) it would be regular procedure to query the social adjuster or the perpetual census before even talking to him. Now he will appear as just another prole without obvious mutations. Perhaps he could bluff them; let them think the Readers have another source of power, which enabled him to reach them. There were self-contained units long ago weren't there?"

"Right," agreed Will-jim. "Very awkward and wasteful, but they worked part of the time. As a matter of fact, if we had time, we could duplicate such engines and starve the Bureau out."

"I don't know," said Sven-yorn slowly. "It seems to me they would question our having power; why wouldn't we have used it in other, more obvious ways?"

"There could be lots of reasons," argued Mei-lu. "First things first, you know. Besides, even if they wonder, how are they going to get around the fact that Jo is actually up there?"

"Well," finally agreed Sven-yorn, "I suppose if they *think* we have power it's just as good, from a bargaining point of view, as if we had it. It may be worth a chance."

From the window came the news, "They're trying to rig up what looks like some kind of hoist. Work it by hand. Anyway they're raising it higher all the time by throwing something from a window to the one above, pulling up a gear…"

Ed-jo didn't hear the rest of the report; Lil-isa was whispering, "I'm scared. Suppose you should fall?"

He laughed boastfully. "Me fall? That's a good one. You talk as though you'd never seen me clear a tree with one jump. Why, if I did fall, it'd be so slowly I'd catch hold of something before I went far. Don't be scared for me; just worry about some of the airy notions the Readers have, now that I have a chance to show what I can do."

"What do you mean?"

"Oh, nothing."

He saw her doubtful, anxious look; then he kissed her for the second time. He made his way to the window, pushing aside the watchers without explanation, and swung out through the opening. The sudden prickling under his skin was not fear, but cold; it seemed frightfully cold outside. *If I only had any of the hundreds of thermo suits I've thrown so carelessly in the disposres,* he thought, *I'd never give it up again, but cherish it for the rest of my life.*

He clung to the broken plexiglas and looked down to the great base of the Metro Building. There was a crowd there and he was almost sure some of them were clothed. It would be possible to get back in, write a message, and have one of the suits relayed up. But this would entail delay and explanation, neither of which appealed to him. He shivered again, saw that those below were frantically busy with their project of connecting the vertical line of windows by tossing ropes upward, and bent his head back to look up.

IT WAS only fifteen floors to the first terrace; this would be the easiest part of his climb. The window above had a hole in it, someone was leaning out watching him. "Hang on tight," Ed-jo shouted; "I'm going to have to grab hold of your arm."

The prole looked down puzzledly as Ed-jo bent his knees and let his hams rest on his heels while he hung on with one hand over his head. Then, tensing his muscles, he sprang, giving his body the final push upward with his feet on the plexiglas.

He flew in a slight arc and caught the surprised watcher's arm, almost pulling him through the window. "Hey!" exclaimed the startled prole.

"It's all right," said Ed-jo, releasing the arm and taking a grip on the plexiglas. "Coming up!"

He repeated the jump exactly, again catching an astonished arm, and took off without pause a third time. He was warm now, and exultant; this was going to be easy.

A few floors higher he paused, panting. There was no figure in the window above nor, as far as he could see, a hole in the plexiglas. "What's on the next floor?" he asked his momentary host.

"Next floor?" The face gaped stupidly. "I don't know."

He knew he would face this problem many times before he reached the roof; indeed, after the terrace atop the hundredth floor it would be only by rare chance he found a window with a hole or a watcher. The next leap would merely be the first in a long series; he might as well evolve the technique early.

The windows were practically flush with the quoinium girders between them. There were no unfunctional sills, only the narrowest of projections above to divert some of the rain. The automatic window-cleaners, mere vertical slits with a slight outward flare from which a forced blast of chemical solution followed by warm air was directed against the surface of the plexiglas, seemed to offer no help at all.

"Whatever it is, either there's no one there, or whoever is hasn't any curiosity."

"'Where are you going?'" asked the prole—a little belatedly, Ed-jo thought.

"Roof. I've business with the Plotbureau. Guess it's the window-cleaners for me after all."

"What? I don't get you."

But Ed-jo had already made his leap. His fingers found the flare and he clung, but there was no hold for his feet, nothing on which to brace himself for the next jump. Disappointed and humiliated, he dropped back to the floor below. If there were only some other way of getting up, just so he could avoid the disgrace of acknowledging how idle his boasts had been.

"Something wrong?" asked the prole at the window.

Ed-jo swallowed his exasperation. "Everything. I've got to think. Give everything for a hammer or an ax."

The prole said casually, "Be just the same to you to come inside to think? My arm's getting kind of tired from your hanging on to it."

Ed-jo laughed apologetically. "Sorry. Sure." The hole was too small for him to squeeze through; he tore out shards of the plexiglas to enlarge it.

"Some muscle," remarked the prole admiringly. Ed-jo looked at him sharply, but his face was open and sincere. Evidently, the conditioning, which was supposed to instill revulsion against physical exertion, had either been unsuccessful or had been overcome.

As his pupils dilated, he saw that this was one of the factory floors; a series of long conveyor-belts, glass-enclosed, ran parallel along the floor. Between the rows were the couches, telescreens, servadors and disposers of those who ministered to the machines. The proles gaped at him with uneasy curiosity. They were all shivering from the

71

unaccustomed contact with the normal temperature of the outside air.

"What's made here?"

"Thermo-suits. This is the finishing department. If we only had some way to get at them—"

"Why don't you break the glass?"

"With what—our hands? The belts are enclosed in triple safety-glass; the machinery is fully automatic; we can detect imperfections through the glass and make adjustments, but we can't touch the finished product."

Ed-jo shrugged. His hope of finding a heavy object that he could swing on a rope ahead of him to break the windows above as he climbed would not be fulfilled here. He glanced at the shivering proles and proclaimed loudly, "It's going to be all right. I'm on my way up now to tell the bosses they can't get away with this."

HE WAS not entirely sure the answering murmur was respectful. Hurriedly, Ed-jo added, "All I need is some way of getting a foothold on one window in order to jump to the next."

They looked at him uncomprehendingly. Finally the prole who had been at the window asked, "Why don't you follow the line of windows where the air-intakes are?"

"Air-intakes?"

"Sure. Where the fresh air comes in for conditioning."

Ed-jo felt deflated and foolish. "You know where they are?" he asked humbly.

"About ten windows over, I think. Can't tell from the inside."

He broke out the indicated plexiglas. "Don't see any sign."

He withdrew his head and the prole looked out. "Next one over."

This was already broken; Ed-jo enlarged the hole and climbed out. The intake-vents were inconspicuous, streamlined downcurving prisms, offering the barest minimum of dubious, slippery foot-hold. Nevertheless he was elated to feel the slight ridge beneath his toes; no normal, Earthborn man could possibly have used it as a leverage.

He bent his knees and sprang upward. His fingers caught in the cleaning-vents of the window above; his feet found the next intake. "This is going to be a cinch," he exclaimed aloud.

A few more leaps brought him over the parapet and on to the terrace of the hundred and first floor. Without pause he began scaling the cliff of the fifty stories to the next setback.

CHAPTER EIGHT

ONLY RARELY now were there broken windows with watchers framed in them. The illusion that four hundred leaps was a mere arithmetical extension of one was thoroughly dissipated before Green Ed-jo reached the hundred and tenth floor. The pads of his fingers were swollen and bruised; soon they would become numb and bleeding. In spite of his resistance to the gravity of Earth, his body ached with the effort.

With each jump, the notion that there was an easier way to reach the top fixed itself more firmly in Ed-jo's mind. No matter how often he considered it, discussed its illogic with himself and dismissed it, it persisted, ever stronger and more nagging. Surely the elevator-shafts... It did no good to tell himself that there was no way of breaking into the shafts, through power-operated doors now adamantly closed, even though he was sure there was no advantage to be gained even if he got inside. The picture of a jammed door, just one in all the multiple banks, in five hundred floors, attained the proportion of a feverish hallucination. If he could only find that jammed door...

The obsession made him stop frequently to pound with a futile fist on unyielding plexiglas as he clung precariously with the other hand and the faint toe-hold. But his hammering had not sufficient force to crack the tough compound.

The second terrace—that of the hundred and fifty-first floor—was at once a glorious, unbelievable achievement and a devastating premonition of failure. It had taken his full endurance to get so far; it was impossible to believe that he could climb three hundred and fifty more stories.

When his breathing had returned almost to normal and he ceased being conscious of the hammering of his heart, he staggered over the width of the terrace and fell against a window. Hardly aware of what he was doing, urged by the obsession which had plagued him through his climb, he beat his fists on the plexiglas, heedless of bruises.

If he had not been half-dazed, the pain would have made him stop before the window fractured; as it was he persisted until the material yielded and broke, sagging inward. Tearing at the obstinate stuff, he finally climbed inside.

In a tiny cubicle, barely large enough to accommodate the oversize couch, the bodies of a man and a woman lolled bonelessly. An overpowering, sweetish, sickening smell lay heavily on the air. Ed-jo gagged at it, attempted to control his nausea, and leaning out the broken window, failed.

He had no idea whether the bodies were alive or dead. His primary thought was to get away from the horrible stench out into the untainted air. But he had caught sight of food, unfamiliar, broken and scattered, but nevertheless recognizably food, on the couch and floor. He was without appetite; indeed the idea of eating was revolting, but on a purely intellectual plane he knew that it was essential for him to gather up some of the scraps. Food was going to be a scarce and precious commodity.

Back on the terrace at last, his hands filled with the odds and ends of a meal, he breathed deeply and reflected on the scene he had just quitted. There was no doubt the room was part of a complex—unquestionably the final part—wherein the Happy Despatch was given to its nominees. He could not classify the smell as that of stale alcohol or opium, but he knew instinctively that it represented a force, which had robbed the two of their sensitivity and normal fears before drugging them with vivid, pervasive dreams. Only the shutting off of the power had interrupted the climax, which undoubtedly would have been the introduction of a lethal gas followed by incineration and automatic disposal of the remains.

Reflections on the grisly aspects of the Happy Despatch were out of place at the moment. It was essential for him to concentrate on the unexpectedly found food and the climb. He put a handful of the broken meats into his mouth.

The astonishing thing was not that it was totally unlike the scientifically-balanced rations that were dispensed from the servadors at Firstfeed or Nightfeed—Ed-jo expected this. What surprised him was that he had tasted similar food before—at the settlement of the Readers. The very appetites which the subjects of the Bureau were intensively conditioned to shrink from and regard as obscene were those catered to in the deathly feast which was supposed to mark the zenith of human ecstasy.

He crammed the last of the food in his mouth and rose to tackle the hundred and fifty-second floor.

ON THE terrace of the four hundred and fifty-first story, Ed-jo fell face-downward, his nostrils clogged with the sulphury odor of suffocation, his lungs gasping harshly for the sandpapery breath that hurt his mouth and throat, his heart slamming itself, terrified, against his ribs. It was no longer a source of pride—it had not been for long, long hours—to reflect that half the strain would have burst the heart and lungs of an ordinary man, one who had not miraculously adapted himself in the womb to the gravitational pull of Jupiter. Ordinary—or extraordinary, he was through; he could go no further.

The Readers would have to surrender now: he could not make those final fifty floors to the roof. His half-formed vision of a new world, midway between the hopeless rigidity of Beaural inertia and the irresponsible, directionless goal of the Readers, with himself as founder and mediator, would have to die before it ever reached the embryonic stage. Wretched, he fell into a gasping doze of exhaustion.

When he jerked into wakefulness it was dark and miserably cold. He shivered, groaned, looked up at the looming bulk above and at the icy stars. The wind seared his flesh, he *had* to climb now, if only to get warm.

His muscles protested as he sprang for the window; fear shook him as he realized that he could not see the vents and had to trust to chance and touch. He clung to the four hundred and fifty-second floor in despair and terror.

Ten stories higher, Ed-jo missed the vents entirely and fell back, clutching desperately. The smooth curves eluded him; with panic he visualized his smashed body on the terrace below. Then he caught and held on to the window washing-slits, utterly beaten.

He could perhaps break a window and crawl in to whimper and twitch in shame and defeat. That he was now in the domain of the top classifications, and that he would be faced by an implacably hostile presence didn't seem to make a difference one way or the other. The ancient—it must be ancient, for he remembered it vaguely as something out of the distant past—obsession of the jammed elevator-door flitted across his mind. What...what... Oh, yes...break open a window. It seemed almost as great an effort as to order his cramped limbs to jump again.

Now the sweeping overhang of the roof loomed above, hiding the stars. From this great projection the threads that were the bileways webbed out toward the other buildings. To reach the edge of this exaggerated cornice was impossible.

Impossible... The whole adventure was impossible from the start. He had known of the overhang and calculated a way of surmounting it. What had it been?

He made the last jump to the top window just under the jutting platform. He hammered at the surface with one hand—hammering, hammering, hammering. Nothing gave; the plexiglas was impregnable.

Suddenly he found he was no longer pounding; his fist had gone through. Dazedly he enlarged the hole and climbed in. Then he stood trembling for long minutes before he collapsed on the floor.

INSTEAD of sinking into unconsciousness, Green Ed-jo found his mind working feverishly. If he were lucky, he would find himself in a hangar, with a ramp giving directly on the roof. Standing shakily he began walking slowly, with hands out before him to avoid stumbling against a stored helicopter.

Instead he came abruptly against a smooth wall stretching blankly ahead. He had evidently entered on one of those corridors, a feature unknown on the lower floors, which gave access only to the banks of elevators and the escalator to the roof. He realized now that no window giving on the hangar would have vents—hangars were not air-conditioned.

A corridor meant electronically-operated doors. His impossible climb had terminated in another impossibility.

Ironical, implacable corridor! There was no point in attempting anything further.

No longer afraid of stumbling over an obstacle, he walked ahead, fingertips against the wall. The darkness was absolute; at no point was there any impression of light, however faint.

He walked for what seemed an interminable time, and a distance, which should surely have brought him past the doors and close to the other end of the hall. Even as he told himself that time and space multiplied to his senses in the dark, he realized with sudden dismay that he should have been able all along to see the faint glimmer from the window at the opposite end of the corridor. There was none. There never had been any.

He knew that all Beaural architecture was precisely symmetrical. Each setback was balanced by others, at exactly the same distance apart; no corridor ended in an unfunctional cul-de-sac. It was impossible that there should be a hall with a window at one end without one at the other.

In spite of the cold, Ed-jo felt his hair prickle with sweat. He turned his head back to gauge the distance from the window into which he'd climbed. It was no longer visible.

Absurd. No matter how far he had come he should be able to see some trickle of light behind him. Was it conceivable that this was some trick of the Bureau's? That he had somehow stumbled into a trap? In panic he began running, then saw ahead not far off, the faint light of moon and stars.

More disturbed than ever, he approached warily. Somehow, inconceivably, he must have got turned around— But even as he formulated the theory he knew it was invalid, it did not take the unbroken plexiglas to confirm it. This was—even though it could not be—the window at the other end of the corridor.

His knees went weak with relief as he finally understood: The corridor was curved.

Ed-jo leaned against the wall feeling his heartbeat slowly return to normal. Then he realized he was no nearer his goal of the doorway; it had eluded his fingertips as they felt along the curving wall.

And of course it would, just as the elevator-openings would. All doors were smooth and flush, machined precisely to show no crack, give no hint of their presence. With the power on, the approach of a person or a robot would activate the electronic eyes, which would then drone, "Elevator going down, please call for a car," or, "Escalator to the roof; please give the password in order to exit." There was no need of any visual indicators when they were replaced by audible ones.

Well, he must figure out the location of the doors without anything to go by except logic, neither touch, taste, smell, sight nor hearing would help. Stop and think. Think hard, for everything depended on his thought.

Symmetry. He was pretty sure there was only one set of doors leading to the escalators from each corridor. That must mean they would be placed in the exact center. If he paced off the distance from window to window, and then retraced exactly half of it, he would come to the doors. What would happen then—would happen then.

ED-JO DECIDED to guide himself along the other wall, the one with the concave curve; he was convinced it was in this that the doors were. Very carefully, he placed his right heel snugly in the rounded corner where the floor joined the wall under the window. For the last time he reminded himself that his paces must be full—the total stretch of his legs—this would be the only way he could make them approximately even.

"One...two...three..." It was absolutely essential to count out loud, firmly and with full attention. Otherwise he might miss, or count one twice over. "Twenty-six...twenty-seven..." Why had he been so sure the doors were on the outer curve? "Forty-four..."

"A thousand, two hundred and three...thousand, two hundred four..." Endless, endless, infinite curve. The opposite window jumped into sight. "Thousand, two hundred sixteen...thousand, two hundred sev—" Crack! His foot hit his goal ill the middle of an uncompleted pace.

A thousand, two hundred sixteen and a half. Half of that was... Ordinarily he would have gone to the nearest telescreen and asked Information; now, having to do the simple operation in his head, he wished he had been more respectful of the books and methods of the Readers.

Six hundred eight and a fraction paces back. And if he had miscounted, or varied the paces... He shut his mind and strode on.

The wall halfway between the windows—if it really was halfway; if his paces had been equal and his arithmetic correct—seemed no different in composition or texture. Tapping produced no variation in echo. Desperately he rammed his shoulder against it, knowing how futile the effort was.

Again and again. Ed-jo drew back, panting. Could the doors be on the other side after all? Or a few feet to one side or the other? Was he bruising himself on unyielding quoinium? Or was it simply impossible, as both his common-sense and scraps of knowledge told him, even for one with Jupiter-born strength to force a mechanism constructed to be impervious to anything but the sound of the password to which it was set?

Again he tried and this time he thought he felt something give. Was his imagination playing tricks? Driving the battered shoulder in spite of uncontrollable wincing, he crashed with all his might. This time there was no doubt he had found the doors and was forcing them open. Forcing? The persistent vision of jammed mechanisms that had haunted him on his climb had materialized at long last.

The night air chilled his sweat as he climbed the petrified escalator. Now all he had to—

"Give the password please," ordered a guard.

Ed-jo almost laughed at the absurdity of it. "Listen, idiot: the power has been shut off by the Bureau, the whole world is waiting to learn if this social system will survive or if we'll have a different one—and you ask me for the password. Just as if you weren't cold and hungry and scared yourself."

"Orders are orders; no one is allowed on the roof without the password."

"Well, I don't know it. And I don't give a damn for it."

The guard said stiffly, "I shall have to detain you until the power goes back on, and I can get instructions from the social adjuster."

"Suppose I refuse to be detained?"

"I don't understand?"

"Oh, it's quite simple; I'll just walk past you."

"But you can't do that. I'm detaining you by instructions of the Plotbureau."

Ed-jo began walking toward the roof edge.

"You can't do that. No one can refuse to obey a Beaural order."

"Can't they? Well I am doing it." Ed-jo turned his back on the guard and surveyed the darkness that was Lank. He did not realize, till this moment, how much he depended on the now silent tele-formers. He knew the direction of his goal, but without the mechanically activated voice repeating, "This is the bileway to the Beaural Building," it was hard to decide which of the three viaducts spanning outward was the one he wanted.

His straining eyes were bothered by a dim, low hanging star before he recognized that it was not a star at all, but a light. An artificial light; not low in the sky, but high in a building. How foolish he had been not to understand that the bosses' preparations for the shutdown of power must have included some means of illumination. And warmth too, no doubt, he thought, shivering angrily.

With the dismayed shouts of the guard still urging him to return and be detained, he set out of the bileway, which must lead to the light. As nearly as he could reckon, it was about four miles to the Beaural Building. A jeecar could make it in a couple of minutes, but jeecars like everything else depended on transmitted power.

He had never noticed before that the bileways swayed and swung in the wind. It gave him a momentary queasy feeling to think of the ground a mile below with nothing but the deceptively slender ropes of woven metal supporting him. One never bothered over such things in the swift progress of a jeecar.

CHAPTER NINE

GREEN ED-JO began running. The greater part of his journey was done; the insurmountable obstacles had been surmounted; what remained was trivial. And he was the only man in the world who could have accomplished it. Not Will-jim with his hoarded scraps of ancient knowledge, nor Sven-yorn, smugly satisfied in his wisdom. Not the Readers with their aspirations, nor the bosses with their power. Not Lil-isa, dark provocation from an alien world. Only he.

The light ahead was not a single one, but several in a row, coming from near the roof of the Beaural Building— undoubtedly the next to top floor, the bosses' quarters. Without effort he made his fast pace still faster.

He brushed past the guards on the roof, jeering. The Bureau's single weapon was the conditioning; when that failed, or was neutralized, the Bureau was helpless, having given up the use of force. The Readers' weapon was natural aversion to the dead end the Bureau could not help working toward. If Ed-jo had anything to say about the future, there would be a compromise—and that compromise would not disdain the use of force when it was necessary.

He avoided the escalator for the ramp to the storage-hangar, trusting the bosses would have left a way open from their quarters to the roof. Feeling his way cautiously along the wall, he was rewarded with sudden emptiness where a door had evidently been propped open. And as he had dared to hope, his eye caught the faint gleam of a light.

The elevator-shaft was open; a crudely-fashioned ladder rested on the roof of the car which was level with the floor below. But it was the light hanging in the shaft that held his attention, for this was nothing more than a bowl of oil in which floated a burning wick. He was equally-impressed by the primitiveness of the device, and the evidence it offered that the bosses had prepared long and carefully for their stroke.

Ed-jo went down the ladder and started along the corridor, dimly-lit by lamps flickering in the rooms whose usually-invisible doors were wide open. He caught glimpses of figures, erect and recumbent; paused and then, for no reason he could name, went on a few doors further.

"I want to see The Boss. Smid Jor-al."

TIIREE MEN standing about a couch turned, startled toward him, revealing the stout individual reclining who scowled in his direction. Ed-jo saw that all were clothed in thermo-suits and his anger at their methodical preparations—which assured that the proles should suffer the very lacks the upper classifications had guarded against—was tinged with a certain amount of admiration.

"Who the devil are you and how did you get here?"

Ed-jo was reasonably certain the man on the couch was The Boss. Leaning negligently against the doorway with a nonchalance he did not feel, he said lightly, "Oh, there are ways." He let the sentence hang on the air. *Bluff*, Sven-yorn had said, *bluff*. "You didn't think the Readers were caught entirely napping by your stroke did you?"

The four bosses exchanged looks. Then the man on the couch said smoothly, "No doubt that's why the lights are back on in the prole quarters; we wondered."

Ed-jo could not refrain from jerking toward the window. But the plexiglas was unbroken; there was nothing to see. It was indeed possible that the Readers had rigged up some kind of auxiliary power for the lower floors; on the other hand...

"Probably an optical allusion," he said casually. "We've been too busy with other things."

The bluff was not working. He could see this in the relaxed attitude of the others; he could almost hear the release of pent breaths. Desperately he tried to regain the initiative.

"You might as well let me have the password. Technicians are constructing new circuits around Information. When they are complete, you will be left up here powerless in both senses of the word."

Smid Jor-al yawned. "Please go away; we're busy."

Ed-jo looked around the room as though to find something to spur his invention. But there was nothing inspiring in the limp tangle of metal lying in a corner, obviously a robot who had collapsed when the power went off. Nor in the pile of pemmican wafers and cans of water; supplies for the siege. Nor in the queerly shaped sack that looked as though it had been dropped carelessly against the wall.

"You—" he began automatically, without the slightest notion of what he was going to say, his eyes still on the bulky sack. He did not complete the sentence. The sack moved, with a little, convulsive jerk.

"You..." he repeated. There was something alive in the sack.

"Excellency!" exclaimed one of the men urgently, "The intruder is quite interested in our...hmm...reserve."

"Indeed," said Jor-al. "Well then, we shall have to insist on extending our hospitality to him for the—what's the old word?—for the duration."

Ed-jo tried to keep his voice steady, with just a hint of loftiness in it. *Bluff,* Sven-yorn had said. "I'm afraid it's too late, gentlemen. The Readers already know what you plan, and how you have violated your own basic rule of civilization against the use of force."

"The rule has never applied to hu—"

"Shut up, Obin!" Jor-al cut him off in mid-speech. "You talk too much. Young man, you are quite right in what is obviously a sheer guess. We have had to use force on one occasion, so we certainly won't have any scruples in using it to keep you here. Grab him!"

But Ed-jo's mind was working furiously. Whatever was in the sack was vital to the bosses. And it was not, as he had wrongly guessed, a Reader who was being held as a hostage. The rule against the use of force was, never applied to hu...the boss called Obin—that must be Obin Cyr-Eu, Boss of Mask—had started to say. Hu...hu...what was the rest of the word Obin had choked back?

OBIN AND the other two bosses edged between him and the door. Trying to give the appearance of being concerned only with avoiding them, Ed- jo moved closer to the sack. "Humanoid!" He almost shouted it aloud. That was the only word that fitted. There was an Ishard in the sack; since Ishards were not considered human there was no interdiction on using violence against them.

"You're making a mistake, Smid," he said to The Boss. "Perhaps you are prepared now to use force on a human but your underlings don't relish it. Better reconsider before it's too late. *The Readers know what is in that sack.*"

"Indeed? How interesting."

"You think I'm fooling, I'm not. If the Readers were to give up, you'd have the sack thrown from the window. Its contents are the password to save Information from destroying itself."

The Boss suppressed a yawn. "May I interrupt your imaginative tale long enough to inquire why the power isn't on in that case?"

"You know as well as I do, since you were the one who said that the object would be deliberately ambiguous. The Readers are not yet sure whether the password is to be 'Isha,' 'Ishard', or 'Humanoid'. When they determine, the power will go on—but not on the upper floors."

The Boss sat up and looked at Ed-jo as if really seeing him for the first time. Finally Jor-al asked, "If this is true, why have the Readers sent you?"

Ed-jo debated how much of the truth to tell. This is turn rested on how much The Boss knew of the Readers. He decided to gamble that Jor-al's knowledge was superficial. "There are two groups among the Readers," he declared at last. "I am the leader of one."

"He lies, Your Excellency," burst out Obin Cyr-Eu. "The Readers do not have leaders."

"Be quiet, Obin." Jor-al stared at Ed-jo. "Well?"

"Power," said Ed-jo casually. "It's human nature to want power." He wondered whether he should elaborate on this; thought he caught a faint nod from The Boss, and decided he had said enough. "The group I represent, while agreed to the aims of all the Readers, is not happy at the prospect of a chaotic world. We feel that it would mean the end of civilization."

There was no question of the interest in Jor-al's eye now. I've got him, thought Ed-jo, exultantly. "We have a deal to offer you."

"Impudence!" shouted one of the bosses. "A prole doesn't bargain with the Plotbureau."

"Shut up, Wels," ordered The Boss. "Go on."

"Give me a thermo-suit," demanded Ed-jo. "I'm cold."

Again Wels' sense of propriety was outraged, but Jor-al tolerantly nodded. "Get the Reader-leader a suit." The third boss left the room quietly. "By the way, what's your name? Reader-leader has a jingling sound, but it could turn into a tongue-twister."

"Green Ed-jo."

Ed-jo's confidence continued to grow as he slipped into the warm clothing. The Plot bureau was in the hollow of his hand; one of the bosses had waited on him like an obsequious robot. What a story he would have to tell Jim and Hans and Isa.

"Trouble with the Bureau," he pronounced judicially, "has always been indecisiveness; you never could take a firm stand and stick to it."

JOR-AL SAID, "Very interesting, Green. Sometime I'd like to hear your views on other philosophical points.

Meanwhile, if you could bring yourself to it, we are still waiting for enlightenment."

"Briefly, as things stand, the Plotbureau is through. The Readers will turn on the power and there will be nothing you can do about it. There are no conceivable circumstances under which the Bureau could recapture its old, absolute dominance; but by compromising now, you can save your leadership and a great deal of actual power."

"That is an argument, not a proposal."

Can't stall any longer, he thought. *I'll have to chance everything now.* Aloud, he said. "Our proposition is one of alliance. We will turn the power on—everywhere—and support the leadership of the Bureau against the anarchic Readers. You will see that no obstacles are put in the way of perfecting the machines; we will undertake to stop cheating the Happy Despatch. We will revise our fundamental concepts to permit a limited use of force when unavoidable. Nothing much else need be changed except the outlook on both sides. We shall have, for instance, to consider the desirability of colonizing both Orsog and Isha with our surplus populations—"

"Regardless of the wishes of the inhabitants?"

"Regardless of the wishes of the inhabitants," repeated Ed-jo firmly. "After all, they are merely humanoid. Now, in return, there will have to be one alteration in the structure of the Plotbureau. I shall become its permanent chairman."

"'Permanent chairman'," mused Jor-al. "A mere trifle, eh?"

Ed-jo's mind was divided in half. Part trembling he waited for the Bureau's decision—would they really give in? Really make him boss of The Boss? The other half frantically planned methods of persuading Readers with the technical knowledge to turn the power back on to support him in his wild scheme. He had no doubt that once this was accomplished and he was established in power—

"You may take this absurd imposter away and tie him up," The Boss' voice came smoothly to his astonished ears. "I think the use of force against him is excusable in any case, and particularly since he himself has advocated it."

Ed-jo stepped back against the wall. The doorway was crowded. Evidently some signal had gone out for reinforcements; probably when the boss had gone to fetch his thermo-suit. "You'll have to catch me first," he said.

They showed no immediate inclination to advance upon him. Something pulled his eyes toward the momentarily forgotten sack. It was still wriggling.

Here was an ally at a moment when he desperately needed one. Without turning his back, he retreated toward the sack and with a quick motion pulled at the cord, which tied its mouth.

"Stop him! Hurry!"

But they came very slowly, reluctantly. *Victims of their own conditioning,* he thought, fingers still busy; *they can hardly bring themselves to offer violence.*

The nearest boss advanced with outstretched arm. Ed-jo kicked him in the stomach. He backed away, groaning. Ed-jo succeeded in unloosing the cord.

THE NEXT—and larger—wave of assailants grabbed his legs, tripping him forward. Ed-jo jerked the mouth of the sack open and spun around, using his fists like hammers against the faces of the bosses. Out of the corner of his eye he saw the Ishard shake himself free of the sack. There was a gag in his mouth; his hands and feet were tied. Nevertheless, he managed to stand upright, showing himself slightly shorter than Ed-jo, dressed in a peculiar costume consisting almost entirely of a skirt, with an ornament of some kind hung around his neck by a thin chain.

Unceremoniously, he grabbed the Ishard around the waist and dragged him to the head of The Boss' couch, trusting that reluctance and the last repulse would give him a momentary breathing spell. He knew that if the bosses persisted they could finally overwhelm him; in the meanwhile he was depending on their real abhorrence of violence, and the deliberately-encouraged life of indolence as against his habit of manual work outdoors.

With one eye on the group he worked quickly at the cord on the Ishard's wrists. It had been clumsily, though tightly tied; it yielded quickly.

Just as he got it loose the combined assault struck him. There was no question that this one was of an entirely different quality. For the first time there was determination and cooperation in the attack. He dodged, squirmed and endeavored to shrink out of reach, though in the limited space this was manifestly impossible. Suddenly The Boss shouted, "The humanoid—get him!"

The Ishard, once his hands were free, had employed the moments when attention was concentrated on Ed-jo, to untie the cord at his ankles and rid himself of the gag. Now, having sidled around the scuffle, he was calmly walking through the doorway to the corridor.

Ed-jo slugged into half-relaxed bodies, then leapt over the struggling mass in a bounding arc. "Come on!"

Together they ran toward the elevator shaft with the others in pursuit as they crowded through the door. Shouts from behind urged the stopping of the fugitives, but the occasional head that thrust itself inquiringly outward had an expression too startled or puzzled to suggest quick implementation of any flank attack.

"Here," directed Ed-jo. "In the elevator-shaft."

The Ishard followed him. The door was still jammed open, the primitive light still burned, but one of the bosses had thoughtfully removed the ladder.

CHAPTER TEN

QUICK—ON my shoulders."

The Ishard looked bewildered for a moment as Green Ed-jo stooped; then he climbed on his back, steadying himself on the walls of the shaft. Grasping his ankles, Ed-jo stood erect. "Hang on to the sill," he ordered.

"I...can...not," answered the Ishard, as though he were having difficulty not only with his position, but with the language.

"You must." Straining the muscles of his arms, Ed-jo boosted him another six inches, was rewarded to feel a lessening of the weight as the Ishard's fingers must have grasped the sill above. "Just hang on," he repeated. "I'll pull you up."

The pursuers were now at the elevator. Dodging the nearest, he made his now characteristic vaulting jump, clung for a moment beside his dangling companion, and then pulled himself up over the ledge.

"Guards, guards! Stop them!"

He leaned over and took the Ishard's wrists. But when he pulled there was sudden resistance; those below had caught the hanging feet. There was a yell of triumph.

"Kick out," he panted. "Kick yourself loose."

"Can...not...use...force."

"Damn it, man—this is no time for fancy scruples. They would have killed you—thrown you out of the window alive."

Obstinately the Ishard said, "Die better than force."

Exasperation filled Ed-jo. How could anyone be so blindly fanatical? He had an impulse to let the man from Venus go, to leave him to his fate—and an equally strong impulse to rescue him at any cost. He looked around him for some means of help and saw nothing but the lamp, the bowl in which a wick burned in oil, resting on the ledge nearby. Without losing his hold he reached over with one foot and kicked the lamp down on the heads of those below.

Darkness and screams of pain came simultaneously as the hot oil fell upon upturned faces. He jerked, and the Ishard came upward in his grip. Still holding one wrist, he felt his way forward in the direction of the hangar.

Cautioning silence, they walked quietly up the ramp and stood on the roof. In the starlight, the forms of the guards were perceptible, but they did not seem to be moving in their direction. Stealthily Ed-jo led toward one of the bileways farthest from the guards.

Walking rapidly—for there was no sign of pursuit—he considered the collapse of his grandiose scheme. True, he had salvaged one extremely important success—the approximate password for the continued operation of Information—but what he asked himself bitterly, could he do with it? Give it to the Readers, was the only answer, and then sink into obscurity. A pointless ending to an adventure which at one point had seemed to bring him to the greatest position in the world.

THEY HAD covered half the length of the bileway in silence when, shrugging off some of his chagrin, Ed-jo asked his companion, "How come you got yourself all tied up like that in the bosses' home grounds?"

The Ishard shook his head. "Not speak Earth language good."

"I gathered that much already. But go ahead; I'm no grammarian myself."

"From Isha...ship...hear report."

"You're one of the crew of an Ishard spaceship getting a report from your people here."

"Not crew...what you call—let me see—ah, writer."

Ed-jo shook his head dubiously. "Must be an obsolete word: I never heard of it. But go on."

As near as he could make out from the Ishard's recital in a language, which greatly impeded his expression, the expedition had landed some time before, near the city of Nork. Being evidently of an insatiably curious turn, the visitor had not only been intrigued by his first glimpse of terrestrial life, but anxious to see much more of it than he could during the brief stop of the Venerian spaceship. Finding a fellow planetman in the role of one of the crew of a transcontinental rockepult, he had arranged to be picked up on the next trip from Venus, meanwhile, with his mentor's connivance, stowing away on a flight to Lank. When the rockepult berthed on the roof of the Beaural building, he again begged a stay till the return flight, promising faithfully to remain out of sight of the guards. However, his urgent curiosity had betrayed him; he was captured and taken before the Bureau, who immediately recognized the lucky potentialities for their purpose. They had imprisoned him in a room during the final preparations for their coup; just before the power was turned off, he was bound and gagged and tied in the sack.

During his narrative the moon rose; being nearly full, it showed every twist of the bileway's cables. They now neared the roof of another building, which Ed-jo was certain was not the Metro; no guards were in sight; he surmised that they had abandoned their posts for the shelter of the hangar.

"Now all I have to do is figure some way of getting down from here."

There would, he knew, be little point in exploring any of the other bileways; there was no point at which they connected with lower terraces or the seawater conveyor. The thought of reversing his day's climb could not be entertained; his legs turned to water at the mere idea of attempting to cling to the five hundred precarious holds of a downward progress.

While he puzzled, the Ishard raised the ornament that hung around his neck to his mouth and began speaking softly into it, in a singsong speech. After a while he paused, and the ornament metallically answered. The Ishard smiled, nodded, and gave out another spate of words.

"What is it?" asked Ed-jo, when he was through. "Some kind of communication, I know, but where do you get the power?"

"Just toy," replied the Ishard apologetically, "Speak to my spaceship. Back now, they look for me. Come soon. Power...in here." He tapped the ornament.

Ed-jo shrugged. Strange humanoids! They called gadgets beyond terrestrial technology mere toys, and were willing to let themselves be killed rather than employ violence to defend their lives. Incomprehensible. And Lil-isa was one of them; one of them who had trained herself and studied to pass as a human, and had deliberately chosen the portion of a prole when she might have been enjoying a life which must be—to her—infinitely happier...

WHILE SHAU—which was as near as he could make out the Ishard's name—strolled around the roof admiring Lank's moonlit towers and shadowed spaces, Ed-jo pondered again the humiliating defeat he had suffered. For the first time the thought of what reaction the Readers would have toward the course he had contemplated occurred to him. How would they react to what they must consider nothing less than his contemplated treason? How would Jim and Liz and Hans regard him? Or Isa?

Of course, they could not but be grateful for the keyword, which he was bringing back with him—or rather, a clue from which the password could unquestionably be deduced. But in spite of this, wouldn't there always be a barrier between him and the proles? He could imagine, years ahead in the new society which the Readers would erect—and how unconscionably dull it seemed to him—that he would be pointed out in whispers as the man who had been ready to betray Freedom for his own selfish and unworthy ends.

And there would be no escape. His early dream of leaving the cities for the wild country would become increasingly impossible as the Readers spread out from the urban centers, redeveloping and re-employing the long abandoned rural areas. Earth had no place for Green Ed-jo.

Overcome with physical weariness, as well as with self-pity, he dozed into restless sleep. He was startled awake by a strange, premonitory twinge that some momentous event was about to happen. But the moon still hung bright in the sky; Shau was peering westward toward the ocean; nothing was changed.

"Must be time for the Ishard ship," he muttered.

Then, so startlingly that it gave the illusion of a tremendous noise, the lights of Lank came on. Not flickeringly, not one by one, but all together, in a great crescendo. The mile high towers, dark and dead an instant before, revealed themselves in thousands of illuminated windows.

"The power!" he gasped; they've turned it back on!"

They must, he decided, have destroyed Information rather than surrender or take the chance of injuring the millions of proles trapped in their quarters all over the world. Ed-jo shook his head over such wasteful sentimentality. If they had only waited till he got down with the key word.

It was an anticlimax when the flattened spheroid landed on the roof near them. The Ishard spaceship seemed insignificant in size compared with an exmosphlier, which required a spaceport to receive it; it was no larger than a transcontinental rockepult.

He paid little heed to the dark men and women who came out of the ship, nor their exchange with Shau, who was excitedly talking in their singsong language. Disconsolate, he wandered toward the escalators.

"Cameral Building, Lank," the electronic directors informed him as his proximity caused them to operate. "Please give the password for today and the doors will open."

Ed-jo smiled sardonically. Either the Readers had not yet got around to changing the old Beaural safeguards or... Was it possible that they had surrendered to the Bureau after all?

The director patiently repeated itself. It would go on doing so as long as he remained near it. He moved away; the Ishards would probably be willing to take him down to the ground. Without any particular object in mind he crossed the roof to the wide ramp leading to the hangars.

Where the roof closed over the descending incline there was, on both sides, a series of telescreens, erected so that a number of travelers, guards or visitors might simultaneously send and receive messages. These were now all in operation and few of them carried the same broadcast.

THE NEAREST one showed a group of proles busy working on a machine Ed-jo recognized as Lank's Central Troubleshooter. An excited voice said, obviously for the benefit of those listening in, "Adjustments have now been made on all the doors and elevators, jeecars, copters and other devices in Lank so that the giving of a password is no longer necessary to their operation. For some time they will continue to ask for a password, but the dependent mechanism has been short-circuited. No doubt the same operation has been performed by this time in the other cities."

The next telescreen made Ed-jo's heart jump. The background scene was unquestionably Jupiter; there was a background glimpse through the windows of a cosie of the incredible and majestic Jovian mountains; occasionally a servile gook fussed around the recumbent figure of a man on a couch.

"...and I find it hard to believe," the reclining human was saying agitatedly. "The Bureau swept away in an instant...prohibition of the slaughter of goods...no advantage to service in this colony...don't know what to say. On the whole, I think I'd like to return to earth immediately. On the next exmosphlier."

A voice undistorted by interplanetary static asked, "How about your other Organizers? We have now polled about a quarter of the Jovian colonists and the sentiment for return to earth is unanimous so far."

A chorus of voices jumbled themselves together over the telescreen, "Me too." "No Bureau—what's the use of exile?" "Never want to see a gooch again." "Let's go home." "Home...home...home!"

The next screen was also on an interplanetary hookup. The unfamiliar swamps of Isha steamed under the heavy clouds. "...and naturally we appreciate the expressions of gratitude which have come from our brothers of earth as well as their statements that any and all of the sons of Han will be welcomed on that planet. Now the earth, our first home, is free..."

Ed-jo turned impatiently toward the screen showing a section of Information. "It was, of course, a terribly hard decision to make, especially since we were all isolated from each other by the shutdown of power. I doubt if any Reader, anywhere, ever seriously considered the desirability of surrendering to the Bureau; nevertheless, without consultation, how could any of us take the responsibility of letting Information destroy itself?

"I suppose most of you know by this time that our brothers from Isha transmitted the password; *how* they did it is generally unknown yet. Our source of power is atomic; Isha's is magnetic. Many Ishards carry little sending and receiving sets around with them, but except when there is a visiting spaceship from Isha in earth's vicinity their reach is negligible. Those who volunteered to exile themselves on earth to encourage the Readers to build a new society in the shell of the old all had such radios—to use an ancient term; there is no modern equivalent—with them, but for various reasons, some moral (feeling it not right to have sources of help unavailable to the Readers with whom they had thrown their lot), some practical (the impossibility of proles having private, personal possessions without discovery by the teletectors and consequent exposure to the Bureau) they concealed or abandoned them. However, in every city there were concealed close to the most vital machines, sets that could be used in some great emergency. The danger of discovery was discounted by the fact that even if the teletectors noted their presence, or transcribed their words, they would be disregarded either as machine parts of forgotten usage or as the unintelligible gibberish of static or defective mechanism.

"It was these sets which the spaceship from Isha set in operation when the Ishard Shau informed them of his escape from the Bureau. In every case, Readers heard and managed to get one of their Ishard comrades to the spot in order to translate.

"You will all be glad that not only has Information not destroyed itself, but we have gotten from it the successive passwords So that its security is assured..."

Ed-jo thought resentfully: *Never even mentioned that I was the one who rescued him.*

SUDDENLY the sullen desire to justify himself became imperative.

To the tuning apparatus of the telescreen Ed-jo said, "Private communication please. Nore Lil-isa; Eighty-seventh floor of the Metro Building."

It took some time to make the connection; finally she appeared on the screen. "Ah, Jo," she murmured; "how could you?"

"How could I what?" he growled defensively.

"Use force."

"So the damned humanoid had to spill everything. And I saved his life."

"Ah, Jo, Jo. Still talking of humanoids; still acting the primitive man."

"Primitive. Maybe. Anyway, I'd survive under conditions under which these advanced Ishards and Orsogians—yes, and Readers with their fancy notions—would go under. Primitive man; you put the accent on primitive—I put it on *man.*"

There was a silence. It looked as though Lil-isa was crying. He felt obscurely ashamed of what he had just said, nevertheless he was impelled to burst out, "The truth is, there's just no place for me."

"You're right, Ed-jo," Will-jim's single eye looked out of the telescreen. "The Bureau's answer would have been the Happy Despatch. Now there is no more Happy Despatch; it will never be again. But we who are your friends: Isa, Lu, Hans, Liz, have been talking things over. It is almost certain that the Bureau's colonists will all abandon Jupiter. There is, at the moment no reason for the Readers to send anyone to replace them; under the new conditions we shall have room for years, if not centuries on earth. Jupiter is your native world; you alone of all men can walk freely on its surface. Wouldn't you be happier there?"

Ed-jo was overwhelmed by the nostalgic vision of a cosie, and of the grandeur of the giant planet. Of the warmth and comfort of the presence of goochs who had loved him freely without thinking of return. Of a planet where he would be master—not just because there were no competing humans, but because he alone was destined to be master there.

While he was thinking, forming the words on his tongue: Yes, yes! On the next exmosphlier! Lil-isa's voice came softly: "And I'll go with you, Ed-jo—if you'll consider a humanoid."

THE BALANCE of the story of the coming of Freedom, is, I am sure, familiar to all my readers. The day-by-day account of the Readers' progress in eradicating Beaural civilization and replacing it with a genuinely human one was not only piously recorded in a dozen archives, but transmitted to the sister planets of Isha and Orsog as well as the cosie on Jupiter where lived Green Ed-jo and his wife, Lil-isa. Lil-isa was, of course, more or less a prisoner of the degravitated cosie, while her husband roamed freely; but it is not recorded that she ever complained of her choice.

It was she who preserved the records of the Readers' progress as long as she lived and she passed the duty to her children who saw the great day when the calendar was finally changed to After Freedom, when the earth had finally been purged of all that the Plotbureau stood for.

Here on Jupiter we honor and revere the memory of our first mother, our common ancestor. Of course we acknowledge the importance of our first father, Green Ed-jo also. It is from him that we inherit our ability to walk abroad upon the surface of our planet. But we have our reservations. In the common speech, where so much history is preserved, we say to one who shows signs of obstreperous or unsocial behavior, "Well, you certainly have some of the old Ed-jo in you."

THE END

If you've enjoyed this book, you will not want to miss these terrific titles…

ARMCHAIR SCI-FI, FANTASY, & HORROR DOUBLE NOVELS, $12.95 each

D-21   **EMPIRE OF EVIL** by Robert Arnette
THE SIGN OF THE TIGER by Alan E. Nourse & J. A. Meyer

D-22   **OPERATION SQUARE PEG** by Frank Belknap Long
ENCHANTRESS OF VENUS by Leigh Brackett

D-23   **THE LIFE WATCH** by Lester Del Rey
CREATURES OF THE ABYSS by Murray Leinster

D-24   **LEGION OF LAZARUS** by Edmond Hamilton
STAR HUNTER by Andre Norton

D-25   **EMPIRE OF WOMEN** by John Fletcher
ONE OF OUR CITIES IS MISSING by Irving Cox

D-26   **THE WRONG SIDE OF PARADISE** by Raymond F. Jones
THE INVOLUNTARY IMMORTALS by Rog Phillips

D-27   **EARTH QUARTER** by Damon Knight
ENVOY TO NEW WORLDS by Keith Laumer

D-28   **SLAVES TO THE METAL HORDE** by Milton Lesser
HUNTERS OUT OF TIME by Joseph E. Kelleam

D-29   **RX JUPITER SAVE US** by Ward Moore
BEWARE THE USURPERS by Geoff St. Reynard

D-30   **SECRET OF THE SERPENT** by Don Wilcox
CRUSADE ACROSS THE VOID by Dwight V. Swain

ARMCHAIR SCIENCE FICTION CLASSICS, $12.95 each

C-7   **THE SHAVER MYSTERY, pt. 1**
by Richard S. Shaver

C-8   **THE SHAVER MYSTERY, pt. 2**
by Richard S. Shaver

C-9   **MURDER IN SPACE**
by David V. Reed

ARMCHAIR MASTERS OF SCIENCE FICTION SERIES, $16.95 each

M-3   **MASTERS OF SCIENCE FICTION, Vol. Three**
Robert   Sheckley, "The Perfect Woman" and other stories

M-4   **MASTERS OF SCIENCE FICTION, Vol. Four**
Mack Reynolds, Part one, "Stowaway" and other stories

MONSTERS IN THE STREETS?

*"Only if you're drunk!" you say?
…Think again.*

A shotgun blast to the face could change any man's perspective. Jerry Wolfe knew this, and he paid for his new view on life…with his own life.

Will Chester and his comrades were determined to take up Jerry's crusade against an invading Alien scourge.

The only problem being that not everyone could see the interlopers…

CAST OF CHARACTERS

WILL CHESTER

Just an average man, but an average man willing to risk any consequence to rid the world of evil.

COLONEL BEDFORD

This retired Army officer was no loafer. Hardened, leathery and gruff, he was drafted into a battle to save mankind—and loved it!

GEOFF EXETER

Blinded by the luck of the draw—literally—many thought him to be the bravest of them all.

MARION BLACK

This fighting beauty helped inspire her male comrades...some more than others. Could Chester win her heart?

ALEC TALBOT

He'd already lost one arm in combat, but he would never allow that to discourage him in the coming conflict!

DR. JOHN BARINGER

His cynical nature left him unconvinced of the impending threat, but he would not leave his comrades to go it alone.

JOHNSON

Old—Boer War old. Would this polished and proper gentleman prove his worth in the face of extreme combat?

'AROLD SMIFF

He was a "gin drinkin' drunkard," and no one would have survived without him!

BEWARE, THE USURPERS!

By
GEOFF ST. REYNARD

ARMCHAIR FICTION & MUSIC
PO Box 4369, Medford, Oregon 97504

CHAPTER ONE

I STOPPED the black Jaguar beside the crumbling stone balustrade and swung my legs out. The drive was deep in rotted leaves and long-uncleared trash. Above me the ancient castle looked out across the groves of oak and elm and chestnut to the silent moors, like the veritable ghost of Old England itself: aloof, brooding, noble, withdrawn from this hectic modern age into its memories. Blind blank holes of windows stared over my head as I walked up the drive where in a more regal century the carriages of dukes and knights and princes of the blood must have rolled, the big horses of neighboring squires must have pawed impatiently before many a hunt, and lovers in satin and velvet and cascading lace must have strolled and dallied a thousand thousand times.

As I was hauling open the heavy iron-banded door, my foot trod upon something that squashed unpleasantly. I bent down, and in the sick yellow moonlight saw a newly-dead rook, its eyes already pecked out. I shivered, uncontrollably. Then I went in and pulled the door shut.

My electric torch stabbing the darkness before me, I crossed the empty hall and mounted the broad curving stairs. At the top I turned and glanced downward; the great hall was patterned with moonlight, and although there was no furniture of any sort, the whole vast place seemed to crawl and pulse with shapes of menace, of dead-yet-living evil. I shook myself angrily. My nerves were rotten, my mind was bursting with fear. That was the whole trouble—fear, fear and nerves. The only thing to do was act quickly.

I strode down the dank passageway, opened the third door on the left, went into the room and shut the door behind me.

Here the old stone walls were ashine with lights, the air was less musty and far less creepy. Six people were here, standing about or sitting on straight-backed chairs. They all turned to look at me. Nobody spoke. I nodded to each in turn.

THERE was an old army officer, leathered and permanently tanned by decades of the dreadful Indian sun; he wore a short grizzled mustache and a stern, rather stuffy expression. There was a man of about fifty who could not have been anything but a physician, so scrubbed and competent he seemed. There was a youngish fellow with only one arm, and another whose dark glasses sheltered sightless scar-pitted hollows. There was an antique of a man, poker-thin and poker-straight and poker-hard, with a pale face and keen, faded blue eyes. And there was a girl, who had sometimes been described as a summer sky, as a star, and as other things just as lovely and unbelievable.

"What ho," I said, with empty cheerfulness. "Sorry to be late. Let's get at it."

"Will," said the doctor abruptly. "I forbid it. It's madness, it's criminal lunacy."

"Sorry you feel that way, John. We've gone too far to stop here—and we've been all through this a hundred times." I went to the table and sat down briskly in the vacant chair beside it. Truth to tell, every muscle in my body was rebelling, was shrieking to me that John Baringer was right; only my mind still insisted that he was wrong, and I knew that if I dallied for an instant my body would conquer my brain...

I fitted my head snugly against the curious apparatus we had attached to the back of the chair. It was constructed along the lines of an old-fashioned photographer's head clamp. To the table were nailed a number of steel braces, which held a Tower musket, an obsolete firearm primed with black powder and aimed rigidly so that the load would pass within a hair's breadth of my eyes as I sat with my head pressed against the clamp. The musket was already cocked. "Let 'er go," I said, and felt glad that my voice had not cracked into falsetto.

"No!" said John Baringer. "No!"

None of them moved.

"Have I got to do it myself?" I asked, rather angrily.

The retired officer pushed the doctor aside, took two steps forward and laid his hand on the musket. "Ready?" he asked.

"I am."

"Hold hard," he said, and pulled the trigger.

The world seemed to lift up into the air all at once, its foundations tearing apart with a noise like all hell bursting in half; then it slowly toppled down again, and everything was blackness and hot, searing death.

The last thing I remember was the scream of the beautiful girl, she who was as lovely as a summer sky.

CHAPTER TWO

I LAY in the warm bed and for a long time I tried to think of something that I knew I should recall, and at last, after hours of waking and dozing and waking again, I had it; it was the fact that I was not dead. When I knew this for certain I was extremely surprised, in the weak fashion of the very ill. I slept once more, and when I woke again I was stronger and more in command of my mind. I was still a little astonished that I was alive. Then I began to wonder whether I was blind. The knowledge that I would not know about this for some days was intolerable. I yelled angrily, and a cold hand was laid across my lips.

"Gently, Will, gently," said the loveliest voice in England.

Then I knew that I could bear the uncertainty till doomsday, if I must.

"Hello, Marion," I said, brushing the hand with my dry lips. "What time is it?"

"Middle of the afternoon, Will. You've been asleep a long while. It's Tuesday."

"Tuesday. Good Lord, nearly forty-eight hours!"

"Do your eyes hurt?"

"Not much."

"Thank John for that."

"Where is he?"

"Here," said the physician's voice. "We're all here but the Colonel."

"He's in London," said Marion Black, "buying supplies."

"Is Johnson here?"

"Yes, sir," said the respectful voice of the pale-faced old man. "Very much at sea, if you'll allow me, Mister Chester."

"They haven't told you, Johnson?" I asked incredulously. "You must think us all mad!"

"No, sir," said he promptly. "I give you my word I don't, sir. Had it been one or two of you, why then I might fancy you'd gone off your respective rockers, as you might say, sir; but six of you—that's different."

"What do you think, then, Johnson?"

"I think there's something big going on, sir," said the old man. "Something fearfully big. With poor young Mister Exeter blind, and you a-lying here like this—what *is* it, sir? They told me you were the proper one to explain."

"Johnson," I said, grinning, "that's the first time I ever heard your voice express anything but well-bred deference."

JOHNSON coughed and, I imagine, looked at the floor with embarrassment. "Very strange circumstances, sir," he said.

"I shan't keep you in suspense, Johnson, although these callous people have. Are you prepared to hear a nightmare of a yarn?"

"Are you prepared to tell it?" growled John Baringer.

"Oh, yes. I seem to have had a good bit of rest lately." I drank from a glass that Marion put to my mouth, and said, "You remember Jerry Wolfe?"

"Of course, sir."

"You were there the day he came back to the Gloucester Club and was murdered, weren't you?" I knew he had been, but I was feeling my way into the story.

"Yes, sir. I brought him and Mister Talbot here a bottle of Scotch. I saw him killed."

"He told Alec—" Alec Talbot was the chap with one arm; he'd left the other in Europe somewhere, during the latter days of the war—"he told Alec a tale that day, Johnson. It's a wild, incredible, super-fantastic tale. No sane man would believe a word of it."

"No, sir."

"But we six believe it, Johnson."

"Yes, sir. I gather it has something to do with this—"

"This madness of ours. It does. You see, Jerry Wolfe was nearly blinded in India when a Tower musket was discharged athwart, his eyes. The bandages were removed as he was coming home, and he found he could see...could see rather more than most of us can."

"Yes, sir," said the dignified voice. "May I ask what he could see, sir?"

"He could see into Hell," said Alec Talbot quietly.

"HE could see that certain people are not—people," I went on. "Let me try to explain that. He discovered that there are among us many aliens of another race, perhaps from another dimension, or from another planet, or—who knows?

He thought they were out of a different dimension, because he could see silvery lines behind them, which he believed to be that dimension's scenery, as it were. Each of these aliens, these usurpers, as he called them, had stolen a human body, and was using it as a focal point of entrance into our world. Do you follow me?"

"With some difficulty, sir."

"Drop the 'sir', Johnson. We're all plain human beings together in this."

"Yes, sir."

"Well, he could see these alien creatures, but within them, or behind them, he could also see the human bodies they were occupying; the bodies which to everyone else appeared to be quite normal men and women. The bodies apparently didn't contain a human soul or mind or whatever you want to call it, but were only puppets for the interlopers. He sat in Charing Cross Station and made notes on them at one stage of his adventures, and he decided that they were entering this world by usurping the bodies of newly-born children, children of unions between two of them or between one of them and a regular human. See?"

"Vaguely, sir."

"He figured out that after a few of them got into our dimension, through some fluke or other, they found that they could spawn puppet-humans who would become vehicles for others of their breed. They come 'in' by route of birth. Perhaps, Jerry thought, a freak accident generations ago let just one of them into our world, and he put his foot in the door. Now there are multitudes of them here. What was the ratio Jerry calculated, Alec?"

"About seven to six in our favor," said Alec Talbot. "Of course, that was figured within an hour or so at Charing Cross Station. He didn't have a chance to make a real survey. They got him first."

"Yes, they got him. He was so shocked by his discovery that he didn't cover up fast enough, and they found out he could see them. They harried him all over half of England, and finally they tracked him down at the club and shot his guts out."

"He died in my arms," said Alec without expression.

"But Mister Wolfe was shot by men from Scotland Yard and bobbies, sir," protested Johnson.

"That's what they seemed to be, Johnson, to you. Jerry could see them truly. He knew they were the usurpers, using the husks of human beings as points of contact between our dimension and theirs."

JOHNSON coughed politely. "And this is the story he told Mister Talbot?"

"It is."

"And you all believe it?"

"We do. Partly because it tallies up with a lot of queer things, partly because it explains a lot of others. But mainly because we all knew Jerry Wolfe, and he was as sane and decent a fellow as ever breathed tobacco smoke."

"Yes, sir."

"He couldn't see all of their dimension, you understand. It was only where one of them had taken over a human body that the veil was thin enough to be pierced by his blast-warped sight. There was a sort of force-field or something around them, and he could see the beasts and their nearby background of silver lines that ran at an angle of about forty-five degrees. That was all. He killed the human parts of three or four of them, and although he couldn't touch the other-dimensional folk with his bullets, when their human puppets died they were relegated to their own world again. They faded out and vanished, he said. Their point of contact was obliterated."

"I see, sir. I begin to get the picture. These foreigners—" I could not help smiling at the word—"have been infiltrating our island by some means, using our bodies, you might say, as disguises. A dirty bit of business, sir, if I may say so."

"Very dirty, Johnson. Because if nothing is done to stop them, eventually they'll have our whole world to themselves."

Johnson evidently thought this over for a moment. I could hear everyone breathing heavily in the silence. Then, "What do they want with it, sir?" he asked.

"Lord knows. Jerry never asked 'em."

"Ah. It gives one pause, sir."

"It damned well does. It's given us so much pause—the six of us—that we've decided to devote our lives to fighting the usurpers. That's why we're doing this huggermugger business, Johnson. We're duplicating Jerry Wolfe's experience, trying to get our eyesight warped or marred or shifted, or whatever the phrase ought to be, as his was. So we can see 'em, and combat 'em, and send 'em home to their silver-lined wastelands."

"And that's what happened—"

"To Geoff Exeter. Yes. We did the same thing with him that you saw two nights ago with me in the chair. Unfortunately—there's a feeble word!—we bungled some-how. And Geoff is blind."

"YOU get used to it," said Geoff Exeter cheerfully. "It's in a good cause. Better cause than we fought the Nazis for if Jerry Wolfe was right."

"We're banking that he was. We're betting our eyes or our lives, Johnson, that he was right."

"If you'll forgive me, sir, it seems a terribly long chance to take. He might have been addled in the head, or drunk; or if he was right, you may all lose your eyes and never acquire his strange vision."

"We're relying on old Jerry," said Alec Talbot. "You see, at least three of us were at loose ends, with nothing to make of our lives, and our hearts full of bitterness and frustration. It's given us an aim in life. It's given us life itself, by heaven! We drew lots, Geoff and Will and I; Geoff got first try, Will the second, and I lost. I'm to be the third one. Before he was murdered Jerry told me who was all right and who wasn't. He'd seen a few chaps he knew—Will and Geoff and the doctor here, Marion and Colonel Bedford. He bequeath-ed me their names. I rounded them up and beat them with Jerry's yarn until they began to feel a horrid truth in it. Then just a few days ago I remembered that you'd been our waiter at the Club that night, and he'd sat easy and safe in your presence; so we knew you were human too."

"I'm sure I'm very gratified, sir. But what can I do?"

"We don't know. We don't know what any of us can do. But we were only six, Johnson—six against half a world. We grasped at you like a drowning man at a—"

"Straw," said Marion. "Really, Alec, your similes stun me!"

"I was going to say 'bottle of whisky'," growled Alec.

"Do you get the whole picture now, Johnson?" I asked.

"I think so, sir. Just one thing…"

"What's that?"

"Well, sir, what do these aliens look like? I mean, if you can see them?"

"Like obscene nightmares," I said. "Like demons down under the sea. Like anything and everything you can conjure up that's evil and strange and full of hellishness."

"Oh. Quite so, sir," said Johnson woodenly.

"Jerry talked of toads, of sharks and dragons, weird tree-shapes and amoebae, but he made it clear that those were only far-fetched similes." Alec's voice was low; he was remembering his friend, haggard and gray in the face, a ghastly ghost of the man he had once been. I broke in.

"Yes, Johnson, they're a fearful horde. If Jerry was right, they're overrunning us in a manner far more subtle and deadly than any invader ever did before. Which is why we must take these desperate measures. Are you with us?"

"Of course, sir," said the old waiter.

"Why?" asked the skeptical Doctor Baringer. "Why so quick to leap at this fantastic story, Johnson? I've got into the affair over my head, but I'm still not sure I believe in it."

"Well, sir, you might say I'm in just about the same position as Mister Exeter and Mister Talbot and Mister Chester. I'm an old soldier, much too old to be of any use in a regular war any longer; and I still fret for the days of bivouac and battle. If you'll pardon the liberty, sir, I must agree with you that it's a rum go, a very rum go. But if it's true, then I may be of some slight use in the world after all."

"You were a soldier, Johnson?" I asked.

"Sergeant, Boer War, sir. I fought at the siege of Ladysmith and a dozen other engagements."

"I thought the Boer War was a million years ago," said Marion Black.

"Very nearly, miss," said Johnson with a dry chuckle.

"Welcome to the ranks, Sergeant Johnson," said Alec Talbot.

I started to say something, but suddenly was very weary; so instead I went to sleep.

CHAPTER THREE

TEN days later they took off the bandages. The doctor had changed them and examined my eyes a number of times, but always in what was to me total darkness; I believe he used some sort of queer light, infrared or black or what-have-you. I'm not up on these medical and scientific gadgets.

The last layer of gauze came off. Nothing happened. The world to me was all a pinkish-red blurring.

"I can't see," I said. "John! I can't see!"

"Neither can I when my eyes are closed," said Marion, with a nervous choked laugh.

So I opened my eyes.

I saw a tall straight old man, a one-armed chap, a young fellow in dark glasses, a rather stuffy-looking retired colonel, a middle-aged physician with a worried face, and a girl as radiant as a spring morning.

"Greetings," I said unsteadily. "Greetings, little army. Don't look so scared."

Alec Talbot grinned and Marion gulped with relief, Colonel Bedford clapped me hard on the shoulder, muttering something that was probably "Stout fella!" Geoff Exeter said, "you can see, Will? Your eyes are all right?"

"I think so. Yes, there isn't anything but a little fuzziness around the edges."

"That may be the result of the long spell of darkness," said John Baringer, fussing about professionally.

"Well, let's get out and test the old orbs," said I, throwing off the covers. John pushed me back into the pillow.

"Not for a day or two. You've got to regain your strength. Been in bed a long time."

I raged, but it did no good. It was three mornings later when at last I was allowed to leave the old castle—it belonged to Geoff Exeter's family, by the way, Geoff's father being old Lord Joseph Exeter—and go into town, with Colonel Bedford at the wheel of my Jaguar.

We averaged a wild and impetuous thirty-two miles per hour all the way there. The Colonel was a driver of the old, the very old, school, and obviously wished that the sleek little sports car were a two-wheeled tonga. As for me, I fidgeted and mumbled and longed to get behind the wheel myself; I had once clocked the two-seater at a hundred and fourteen m.p.h., and when she was forced to creep along like this, both she and I were unhappy. However, my job was to observe, and so I contained my impatience perforce.

WE circled the village and came in from the opposite end. No one knew we were staying at the long-deserted Exeter Castle, and we meant to keep it that way. It was a priceless hideaway, an excellent G. H. Q. for our planned insurgence.

The village of Exeter Parva contained some three hundred souls, if one included eighteen large placid-faced farm horses and ninety-seven dogs more or less. It was market day. The countryside had boiled into town for a hectic time. You might have scraped more citizens out of the pubs of one short London lane, and heard more noise in Westminster Abbey; but for Exeter Parva it was a gala morning.

We drove down the main street—I believe it was the *only* street, but this may be prejudice on my part—and stopped to let a couple of deeply suspicious cows pass by on either side. "Well?" asked the Colonel.

I had nearly forgotten the purpose of the jaunt. I narrowed my eyes and stared keenly about me. I saw farmers in dull blue and faded gray, women in carefully mended finery, children in everything from Sunday bests to Saturday rags. I saw what one might see in any small village on market day. I saw no monsters whatever. I sighed and gave a weak grin. "Just people," I told him. "Just Englishmen."

He attempted to gnaw his short mustache. "Which means either that *they* don't foregather in small towns, or that *they* existed only in Captain Wolfe's brain," said he meditatively. "Which, mind you, young fella, I don't believe for a minute. If there was ever a sane 'un, Wolfe was he. Besides, he'd served in my old stations in India." He pronounced it "Injuh." He edged the Jaguar forward through what Exeter Parva doubtless considered its heavy traffic. "Or else the experiment didn't work. When you think about it, that's the logical explanation. Whatever happened to the Captain's eyes must have been almighty complicated. Don't understand a tenth of it myself, these dimensions and whatnot, but there it is. Frightfully complex changes must ha' been wrought."

I was too dispirited to answer that. "Let's have a drink," I said. "There's a tavern. At least we can have a mug of ale before we go back."

"Right." He parked the Jaguar expertly if rather slowly. We went into the tavern, which was called The Leathern Funnel.

"Well, gents, what'll it be?" inquired the barmaid affably.

"Two ales, miss, if you please," said the Colonel. It was lucky for me that he ordered. I could not have produced anything but a squeak or a howl. The mugs bumped down before us and I picked mine up with both hands and drank it off like a thirst-mad sot after a month of bread-and-water. Then I aimed myself carefully at the door and put on the greatest piece of acting of my career; I walked casually and without a single stumble all the way to the street. The Colonel came after me.

"What the deuce, Chester! You don't allow a chap much time to enjoy his bit of ale," he grumbled.

I got in at the off side of the Jaguar without speaking and put my hands on the wheel. "Ready?" I managed to ask.

"Here, I'm to drive."

"You are like hell. Get in." He did. "Hang on." I nudged the old girl out of the village and when we were hidden by the first hill I trod on her pedals with all my weight and terror behind my feet. We crashed off into a beautiful eighty M.P.H., which I held or surpassed all the way home. Three or four times he tried to bellow something at me. I ignored him.

When we had flown up the long winding drive I put her into the stables, part of which we had fitted up as a garage. Then I sat there in the gloom and shook with what felt like fever.

"Here, what is it, laddie?" he barked. "What's wrong?"

"Describe the barmaid," I said.

"What?"

"Describe the barmaid."

"Fortyish, plain, thickset, red hands, red face, couple of warts. Pleasant expression. Right?"

"Not exactly you left out a few things."

"What on earth?"

"The green horns, six of 'em, growing out of her face in the middle where the nose should have been. The shifting outlines that looked now like a tree stump and now like an octopus. The pulsing heart of scarlet fire in the belly. The dusky-pink tentacles that pushed the mugs across the bar. The pure *hatred* that throbbed visibly and seemed to feel cold when it got near you. The eyes like bursting orchids full of slimy white worms."

He put his hand on my arm and tightened his grip until his knuckles grew pale. "Merciful God!" he said quietly. "Merciful God!"

CHAPTER FOUR

WE went into the deserted hall of Exeter Castle. "Look, Colonel," I said, "will you tell them about this? They'll be upstairs. Tell 'em that it works, that I can see as Jerry Wolfe saw, and everything he told Alec was true. I'll be all right after a while, but now I want to be alone. I don't want to be hedged in by close walls, or have to talk. I'll just roam around down here for a bit. You tell 'em it's okay, that I'll speak to them later."

"Absolutely." The Colonel was the best stuff there is. "Come up when you feel like it, son." He was gone.

I strolled over to one of the great mullioned windows and touched its dusty glass lightly. That glass was older, probably, than all our little band put together. I thought: when it was placed here, were the usurping devils abroad in England? How long have they been filtering through into our world—a hundred years, a thousand? If you start with one and he lets in others, then figuring by the birth rate and the multiplying branches of his horrid clan, how long would it take to let in a million of them? How many figures of our glorious history were just that—figures, puppets, marionettes pulled by fourth-dimensional strings, flesh-and-bone shadows fronting for demons...

We are no other than a moving row of magic shadow-shapes that come and go...

Jerry had asserted that when the human body died, the alien was relegated to his own world again. Then it had to come back, I presumed, via another birth. It must be centuries, then, at the very least a couple of centuries, since the first one came through. It takes time to corrupt the blood of six-thirteenths of all England.

But was it six-thirteenths? Jerry had taken his census in Charing Cross Station. At Exeter Parva I had seen exactly one usurper. Were they then centered in London? Were there perhaps no more than fifteen or twenty thousand of them altogether? That brought down the odds!

I laughed loudly, and the age-old echoes waked in the oak rafters and laughed after me. Oh, the odds were in my favor, all right.

Opposing me, say (conservatively) twenty thousand foemen: great livid beasts like nothing a sane mind could conceive, that had a system of communication outside my dimension which could gather a score or a thousand of them to down me if I showed fight.

On my side, a regular Colonel Blimp of a retired officer, a Boer War veteran, a skeptical middle-aged physician, a blind man, another chap with no left arm, and a girl.

And I: Will Chester, thirty-three years old, five feet ten, moderately strong, normally intelligent; having all my teeth save two, a thick crop of black hair, brown eyes, a complexion more ruddy than otherwise, and a face that, if it would not halt a charging bull in his tracks, still would not win a beauty competition either... Seven years of Army behind me, an income of eight hundred pounds a year from a legacy, and nothing much in view as a future, until this morning—when I had suddenly been elected the savior of mankind.

I walked across to the tremendous blackened fireplace, empty now of everything but a lonely-looking single bronze firedog. Above the keystone of the arch were the arms and motto of the Exeters, done in ancient stonework. I could not read the motto, having forgotten what Latin I once knew. The arms were a jumble of crossed lances, fleurs-de-lis, and hounds couchant. I wished I had a hound to fondle and pat, to be a companion in these moments when I felt I could not bear a human being near me.

FOR half an hour or so I stood there gazing blindly into the depths of the hearth and pitying myself shamelessly. Then a touch on my arm made me leap like a deer. It was Marion; Marion, carrying with her her own special radiance even in the shadowed hall.

"What cheer, old stager?" she said.

"Not much cheer, lady."

"Obviously. What is it got the wind up? Scared sky-blue-pink?"

"Yes. I've just realized that this whole affair is fact, is true; that it's not a crazy adventure in fancy, but a dreadfully real matter of saving the sane world from destruction—and I'm scared!"

"We all are." She said it quietly, and with her simple words I knew for the first time that I was not alone in my terror of the unknown. We were all afraid. I put my arm around her shoulders. Her long light hair tingled on the back of my hand. I loved her very much, and so I tormented myself.

"I've been thinking of Jerry Wolfe, and of how alone he must have felt. He didn't have six pals behind him when the first alien fouled his view."

"Poor old Jerry," she said.

"You were engaged to him, weren't you?"

"Yes, back in prehistoric times, before Jennifer Tregennis caught him. Jennifer was one of *them,* you know."

"Yes, I know. D'you still love Jerry?"

"How do you mean? Of course I do."

I didn't say anything. She went on after a moment. "But I'm not in love with him, if that's what you're driving at. Good heavens, Will, do you see me as a moony widow-in-name-only? I've got more sense than that."

My heart lifted. I patted her on the back. "Come along young Marion. Let's go plan strategy with the troops."

We went up the stairs to our sitting room and I stood before the six of them and took the reins into my hands. I had a job to do.

CHAPTER FIVE

"IT comes to this, then," said Alec. "You mean to go and mingle with the enemy, and try to discover weak spots in 'em, eh?"

"I don't see any other way to begin. We've been scratching for a plan ever since we first heard of the usurpers; and nobody's come up with one, for the good reason that we have nothing to go on. Oh, granted we know we can kill their worldly bodies and send them home. But I hardly think we're going to do nothing but roam the countryside killing off puppets for the next thirty years."

"Remember what Jerry told me—that once one of them was sent back to his own dimension, he could evidently still communicate with those who were left here? That the aliens who're attached to human bodies exist in both dimensions equally?"

"Yes, Alec, I was thinking of that a few minutes ago. It means that under no circumstances can I let any one of them discover I can see them; for even if I killed him here, he could go around his silver-lined dimension telling all his pals about me. It means working in the dark, from behind, anonymously. It means I've got to be circumspect as Satan. We all have to be circumspect."

"Beg pardon, sir," put in Johnson, "but when do the rest of us have a try at warping our eyeballs?"

"You don't, Sergeant," I said flatly.

"What d'you mean, we don't?" cried Alec. "Of course we do."

"No, son, not for a while, anyhow. It's a hundred to one, or a million, more likely, to one, that we couldn't duplicate the exact injuries again. We can't blind anyone else now.

One of us seeing them may be enough—or if he isn't, then half a dozen might not be any better."

"I think Will's right," said Marion suddenly. She lit a cigarette while we waited. "I think we mustn't press our luck too far. At least we should wait until we have a plan. I think—I really think one will be enough."

"Why?"

"Those million to one odds. Why did the experiment succeed the second time? I think God's with us. I think God's on our side, and means us to win."

We were all very quiet for a while.

I went over to a wall mirror and examined my face. I took out my little tin of pancake makeup, Marion's clever idea, and spread some thinly on the scars of the blast: the little pink almost-healed scars that ran across the bridge of my nose and scattered out fanwise toward my ears. We were dealing with cleverness beyond thought, and every tiny giveaway must be taken care of.

"Jerry Wolfe died," I said, still peering in the mirror, "because he was taken unawares, because he hadn't prepared himself to stay incognito among them. I have. I've had my first sight of *them*, and been terribly shocked, yes; but now I think I'll be all right. I'm ready to go."

"Up to London?"

"Yes."

"We'll all go."

"In a bunch? I don't think."

"No, in pairs and trios. But there's no sense in any of us frettin' here without news from you." The Colonel was firm. "The motors are below. Ready, you chaps?"

"Packed and primed," said Geoff.

"Let's be off."

And almost before I knew it we were in the old stables, putting our gear in the back of Alec's great red Rolls.

"Who'll ride with me?" I asked.

"Not I," barked the Colonel promptly. "I've had some of your idea of driving."

"I'll go with you, Will," said Geoff Exeter. "Just put my fist on the car, will you?" I did so, and he climbed in. "I like speed," he said.

I had been hoping for Marion's company, but Geoff— well, he rated a front-row stall in the game. He'd lost his eyes for us. I said, "Geoff will stick with me for the first days. The rest of you put up at the Albany, where Colonel Bedford has a suite, and at that inn in Baker Street, The Gray Gander. Geoff and I will be at the Gloucester Club."

"I shall be there too, sir," said Johnson. "I've been on 'sick leave' quite long enough."

"Roger. Geoff, the Sergeant and I at the Gloucester. The Colonel and John at the Albany. Marion and Alec at The Gray Gander. Don't get in touch with me, unless you give birth to some really ripping idea. I'll find you when there's news."

I touched Marion's hand in farewell, and slid into the Jaguar. We backed out and shot away into the blue.

CHAPTER SIX

WE stood at the bar of a dingy little pub on the outskirts of the dingy little district of Seven Dials. Geoff, who was learning to orient himself by sounds, heard the clunk of his mug on the bar, and unerringly put his fingers around it. "Pretty good, eh?" he asked me, sipping the half-and-half.

"You'll be a wizard at it in a few months."

"I meant the ruddy ale, idiot, I'm not bragging about my accomplishments yet. Seen any of our chums lately?" he asked.

"Oh, dozens. Run into 'em everywhere." It was a kind of simple code; I was telling him that the pub was full of the aliens.

"Fine. Any of 'em give you any news? Anything startling been happening?"

"Not much. Same old stuff."

Same old stuff!

Same old fiends from Abaddon! Same old hosts of Hell! Same old ogres and ghouls, harpies and bugaboos, hobgoblins and hellhags!

The barman, when I squinted, was a big jovial red-nosed Cockney. The barman, when I opened my eyes normally, was a writhing monster, a shapeless blob of intangible protoplasm in whose depths moved turgid lights of orange and mauve; from whose devilish form the waves of malevolence came and went like the roiled swell made by the sluggish moving of some hideous primeval entity beneath the surface of a grisly tarn...

I grinned at him. "Cool weather for June, mate," said I affably.

"Ar, yus," he agreed.

I was pleased with myself. Like a spy plunked down in a strange land, I had been feeling my way to confidence these last days, growing used to the shapes about me, learning to show an expression of bland normality when confronted with unnamable horrors. I believed I was perfectly ready now to begin our war.

The only trouble was that I hadn't the faintest idea of *how* to begin it!

ONE could move among these usurpers for a lifetime, I thought, and learn nothing about them except that they were more hideous than leprous two-headed baboons, more incomprehensible than might be the dwellers of Mars. I watched them talking among themselves where they sat at the little oak tables. While their earthly husks chatted of prosaic things, the forms around the husks spoke—inaudibly to me—with twisting tentacles, gesturing pseudopods, flowers of rotten-looking "flesh" that grew upon their bodies and swelled and burst and subsided to nothingness again. I knew they were speaking of terrible things…

"Let's go," I said to Geoff. "Time we were thinking of bed."

"Righto."

I gave the barman goodnight in a pleasant voice, and we emerged from that ninth circle of Hell into the cool and lovely air. Seven Dials lay about us, all a-murmur with the homely human sounds of earth's, evening. I could not stand it.

"Geoff," I whispered, "I'm going to start the ball rollin'. I'm going to find out something."

"How, old son?"

"I'm going to do a murder."

"Think it's wise?" he asked.

"I want to ascertain something. Just come along a bit."

We went up a dingy street and turned down a lane or two, until at last we were alone on a length of grubby pavement, shadowed by the rickety houses on either side. "Stand here," I said to Geoff Exeter. "It's black in this corner and you won't be noticed. I'll come for you in half a tick."

He saluted carelessly. What nerve he had! To stand alone, blind and helpless, ignorant of what I meant to do—I think Geoff was the bravest of all our little band.

I slunk up the street to a place some forty yards off, and hid myself in a time-battered doorway. The street lay empty and deserted in the early moonlight. I drew the great keen knife that lived on the side of my belt these days, and I waited.

A man came down the road, staggering drunkenly. He was a man. I let him pass.

Another came toward me. I heard his footsteps in the dark, echoing valley of brick, and shortly thereafter saw him pass beneath a fading street lamp.

Do you remember the passage in Doyle's *Lost World*, where the hero is pursued along a jungle trail by a prehistoric carnivore?

"This beast had a broad, squat, toad-like face...the moonlight shone upon his huge projecting eyes, the row of enormous teeth in his open mouth, and the gleaming fringe of claws upon his short, powerful forearms. With a scream of terror I turned and rushed wildly down the path."

Well, I did not turn and rush wildly down the street, but if I had not been hardened by much contact with the aliens, I think I must have done so. This was the worst I had seen: toad-like, yes, but squat and loathsome as no toad ever hoped to be; and indeed some of the projections of its form did look like claws and fangs. Yet no prehistoric reptile could ever have exuded the repulsive effluvium of evil which radiated from this hideous usurper.

As it passed me I felt my stomach draw in as if from a sharp blow, and it is a wonder to me to this day that I did not scream or become violently ill. The gods were with me, however, and I kept strict silence.

WHEN it had gone on a dozen paces, I slipped out and followed it noiselessly. Moving as I had moved on many a commando raid in the old days, I eased up behind it. It did not turn—neither of its bodies turned. Narrowing my eyes, I lifted the great knife and struck, with all the hatred in my soul concentrated in the blow. The blade sank into the pseudo-human neck, severing the spinal cord instantly, and before my horrified eyes the great toad-creature swelled, turned vivid crimson, and went out like the flame of a trodden candle.

It had left our dimension in the very instant that its human husk had died.

Sheathing the knife under my coat, I flew down to where Geoff stood patiently waiting. I took his arm.

"Come on, boy, let's make tracks."

"Home?"

"No, to another pub." We hurried down an alley, turned up a street and down another, until I had put a maze of lanes behind us. Then we slowed abruptly and ambled into a smoky little room full of liquor fumes.

"Two beers, old toff," I said to the fright behind the bar.

We guzzled them slowly, while I watched the aliens around the tables and at the bar. Shortly there was a flurry of excitement among them, the tentacles writhing quickly and the ghastly brutes enlarging and deflating as though pumped by a bellows. All the time the human portions drank and chatted and played darts. But the usurpers were excited over something. Shortly half a dozen of them moved toward the door, the people in no evident hurry, but their marionette-masters wriggling like mad, as though eaten with impatience.

I knew they were going to discuss something important. I had what I had come for.

"Bedtime," I said to Geoff Exeter.

We went out of the pub and caught a tram for the vicinity of the Gloucester Club.

CHAPTER SEVEN

SAFE in our rooms, with Johnson sitting, very unlike a waiter, behind a bottle of brandy and a tray of sandwiches, and Geoff lying on the Chesterfield smoking a pipe he could not taste, I told them what I had done.

"It's taught me a couple of things I didn't know, and affirmed some others I wasn't sure of. First, I'm certain the faculties of these brutes are the same in this dimension as their 'human parts'. That toad didn't hear me coming, I know. He didn't have time to turn and get a look at me before he went *pop* and left us. He was bound to the body till I released him, I think, and if he'd left it he couldn't have got back into it, or rather around it. His ears weren't keener than a man's, or he'd have turned to see me when I crept up behind him.

"But their communication system is terrific. That's where they have it all over us. When he was shut out of our world, the toad must have gone around their region telling his pals about it; and before long the ones who were in that pub heard of it, too. Now they weren't told by a newcomer, for I watched the door; so they were told on *their* side of the veil, by an alien who wasn't occupying a human frame. Got it thus far?"

"I admit to a little uncertainty here and there, sir."

"Well, put it like this. There's a long tall screen set up across a stage. On one side of the screen—our side—are a lot of human beings. This side is our world as we know it. On the other side, the fourth dimension or whatever it may be, are a lot of these horrid-lookin' beasts of usurpers.

"Now here and there in the screen are holes, and through them some of the aliens are holding fake human beings, just as in our well-worn simile of the puppet show. I can see those who are leaning through the holes, but you can't.

"When they're leaning through, they haven't any powers except those of normal people. They can't hear any better than a man. They can't walk through bricks or see through stones. They can't look behind them without turning the human puppet around. I've been watching them and I feel pretty certain of that. In some curious way they're limited by their puppets' limitations here. That makes it easier to assassinate 'em, by the way—I just have to make sure that the human form doesn't get a chance to turn its head and spot me before it dies."

I drank a little brandy and went on intently. "The only way they really have me beat six ways from the jack is in their system of tidings, of spreading 'em, I mean. That's a marvel. For as soon as I shoot or stab or throttle a puppet, the beast that's been twiddlin' his strings leaves him and goes along behind that hypothetical screen between the worlds, telling all his playmates about it; and if he's had a chance to see me, and can describe me, then about a thousand of the others will be watching through their holes in the screen for a blighter of my specifications, and my name is Lord Jonathan Mud."

"I see," nodded Johnson.

"So my problem is to remain utterly anonymous. And I needn't tell you that if I try to embark on a career of murder-by-night, I won't last very long."

"No, you won't." Geoff was grave. "What else is there to do, though?"

"I don't know. And I think I could watch them for a lifetime and not learn another thing about 'em. I'm a tremendously handicapped spy because I can't disguise myself as one of them, and I can't understand what they say to each other. It's like a man going into a colony of bears and trying to pass himself off as a bear, except that I can't even begin to look like a usurper, while I *could* put on a grizzly skin."

"What are we to do, sir?" asked Johnson. His pale face was deadly serious. "We must do something, sir—but only you can decide what it's to be."

Two weeks before, I might have groaned aloud at such a responsibility. Now I took it in stride. Anyone who had been observing the demons of Hell at their work for fourteen days and nights had either to take things as they came along or to go stark staring loony.

"I'll tell you what we'll do first. I'll take Geoff over to the Albany. Then I'll strike out alone for a bit. Maybe for a week, maybe a month. Travel light, fast, and inquisitive. Give myself a chance to cook up plots. And if nothing's come of it by then, why, I suppose we'll just have to set up an assassination bureau and hope I live a hundred years..."

CHAPTER EIGHT

AND so for a time I dwelt alone among the beast-folk.

Packing a few shirts and such in a Gladstone bag, I left London in the black Jaguar, ostensibly on a casual motoring jaunt. I headed up through the East Anglian Heights, stopping the first night in the lovely town of Bury St. Edmunds. Strolling through the streets next morning, I was astonished and heartened beyond measure to find not a single usurper abroad. I went into a pub—I had begun to think that the aliens were concentrated in pubs, so many horrendous bartenders had I seen—and bought a pint from a perfectly normal girl. Lingering about the town, I passed the time of day with gardeners and workmen and loafers, and was tempted to throw up the game and stay here in this oasis of normality forever; but after lunch forced myself to get into the Jaguar and roar off into the Lincoln Heights, where I spent a jolly evening in Old Bolingbroke talking politics with a spidery yellow creature who amused himself by flicking my face now and again with his hairy-looking, tenuous, unfelt members. When at last I went to bed I felt that I had served my apprenticeship and was a full-fledged spy who could thenceforth bear anything the enemy could show or do...

I worked westward and put up for a week at Manchester, in which great inland port I found an awful concentration of *them*. I left the two-seater at a garage and walked the streets from dawn till midnight, observing, thinking furiously, trying to construct impossible plans of attack.

The third night, making sure that my knife was safely sheathed under my coat, I went into the slums to do murder.

Deliberately I chose my victim: a strapping brute of a navvy whose mortal form was surrounded by a cloudy gray beast of indescribable grossness. I shadowed him from tavern to tavern, finally catching him alone in a narrow gut of an alley where the light fell dismally on scummed pools of stagnant water and heaps of filth. I crept up behind him and circling his neck with my left arm I held him motionless for dragging seconds, my knee in the small of his back. He struggled madly, but could not turn his head; and although the gray fiend puffed up and hurled out its streamers of ugly mist-like stuff, I knew it was helpless to see me without twisting the human neck around. That was what I had wanted to know for certain, what I had staked the continuance of my crusade on. I tipped up the navvy's chin and sliced across his throat with the clean steel. He died, gurgling, and the monster dwindled away into gray ribbons and vanished.

NOW I felt I had verified my earlier theory of the limitation of their senses on this plane. Not only did the outsider have to rely for hearing on the ears of his manikin, for tactile sensations on the nerves of the were-human, for strength on its muscles and (for all I knew) for taste and scent on the poor dumb thing's tongue and nose—but most important of all, I believed that the beast must see into this world through the puppet's eyes, and through them alone! The recent gray devil had been able to twist and turn itself to some degree independently of its fleshly body; what I took to be its eyes, a cluster of violet-tinted globules high in its upper torso, had flashed all round as it moved, even seeming to flit over me once or twice; yet it obviously could not detect me with them, or surely it would have concentrated their baleful focus on my face.

No, I was certain that I could only be seen by the eyes in the heads of the puppets. I may as well say now that I never had cause to change this conception of mine, and still strongly believe it to be true.

This may be as good a place as any to make it plain that my descriptions of the beast-folk are of necessity limited and analogical; but that the beings themselves had no analogy in anything existing on this prosaic three-dimensional globe. This is true in part because of their utterly undefinable proportions and lineations, which had to be seen to be fathomed, and in part because the creatures did, after all, exist in at least one more dimension than our acknowledged three, so that, despite my own mutant vision, I saw them in a state of flux, continuously moving, warping, and seeming to bend at impossible angles and to flow off just beyond the range of my sight into a sphere which was to me forever invisible.

It must be understood, too, that when I identify portions of them as beaks, mouths, orifices, eyes on stalks, and other natural parts of animal life, I am only grasping at the nearest comparison. For all I know, their senses may reside in quite different organs than eyes, mouths, noses and so on. For all I know, indeed, they may have no actual five senses in our meaning of the term. They seemed to communicate, it's true, by a kind of writhing and wriggling motion, which may have been accompanied by sounds which I could not hear; but this may have been akin to a nervous reaction, while their actual talk might well have been telepathic.

DURING the next two nights I gave rein to my intense abhorrence of these invaders from another world, and stalked through the city slaying indiscriminately in a passion of hatred. This makes me sound as bloodthirsty as a weasel. Well, I was. A tiny human David opposing a hideous throng of Goliaths, I gave no quarter even as they had given none to my friend Jerry Wolfe.

Of course the police, the newspapers, the citizens of Manchester were shaken by the wave of inexplicable violence. Headlines shrieked that a new Ripper was abroad. And at that I began to wonder: what if an accident had happened to somebody's eyes back in the 1880s, and he, seeing the aliens all about him, had begun on a wild career of assassination like my own? What if he had prowled the slums as I was doing, killing and mutilating in a frenzy of detestation? Was that the true explanation of the never-identified Jack The Ripper? Was he, perhaps; a much-maligned champion of mankind? It was at least a fascinating possibility!

For those few score of hours I felt no remorse, no distaste for my butcher's job, no sorrow except a fleeting one for the human relatives and friends of these poor brainless husks I was destroying. And their grief; I was persuaded, was as nothing in the balance against the good I was actually doing them by ridding our plane of the invading beast-folk.

Then reaction set in, and I lay in my hotel room and shook as though I had blackwater.

I couldn't keep this up, week after week, month after month, for years—even if I were not discovered, either by our police or by *them*, I knew I could not go on. Give me what resounding titles you wish: savior of mankind, champion of humanity, valiant worker for the survival of the race—I was still only a kind of butcher. I knew I was glutted with killing. The papers put my total score at nineteen corpses. They were husks, puppets, yes; but even though what I killed had no life save that imparted by the guiding usurper, it still had the flesh and the blood of my own breed. When the alien was dispatched to his own place, what remained had the look and feel and smell of someone who might have been my brother. I had once quite callously shot a number of tigers in India; but when a tiger dies, he does not turn into the slashed corpse of a man. He remains a tiger. If only the usurpers had continued in their own true shapes after the slayings, I think I might have gone on killing them forever.

So again I moved harmlessly among my foemen, and watched them colloque together in their silent, loathsome fashion, and did nothing.

And a great melancholy took me; and I felt as helpless as a child surrounded by the dismal wraiths of all ghost-haunted England, as hopeless as a man alone in a jungle full of teeming ghouls.

I would have given a year of my life for one hour with Marion Black, but I would not write or telephone her to come to me. I didn't want *them* to be able to connect me with any of my band, in case *they* ever discovered my identity.

Then, on the last night I spent in Manchester, I got a little drunk (out of frustration and despondency, and my inarticulate, stupidly silent love for Marion) and I decided to put just one more of the enemy out of the fight, before I went on my way.

CHAPTER NINE

IT was a mean street, one of the meanest in the whole city. The moon was vivid, and straight overhead, so that my shadow lay in a black little pool around my feet. I sought a dark doorway and waited, knife in hand, my brain full of liquor and loathing.

A man, and a man, and then a beast…

I slid along in his tracks, glancing quickly behind me to make sure we were unobserved, and swiftly performed the now-familiar operation of driving the impalpable demon back to its own dimension by hacking the throat of the man-shape. Standing above the dead thing, I knew for a second or two the feeling that must have held Jack The Ripper as he stood over his victims: I wanted to stab and slash and mutilate, I wanted to let out some of the terrible hatred that boiled in my heart.

Civilization won, however, and I sheathed the knife after wiping it clean on the man's leather jacket.

At that moment one of *them* came round the corner and stood staring at me, not twenty feet off!

It was a gorgon of a brute, with several repulsive "heads" on lean stalks of necks; the biggest one looked rather like a hippopotamus whose mother had been frightened by a Ubangi, and I was so used to the weird beings by now that, had I seen this one on a daylit street, I think I would have chuckled. In that deserted lane, though, with the shell of its brother's puppet at my feet, I didn't chuckle. I turned and ran like hell.

A whistle split the air; I turned my head as I pelted away, and squinted my eyes. By all the gods! The hippo-gorgon was a bobbie! A ruddy P. C.!

The garage where my Jaguar champed at her inactive gears was only a couple of blocks from the lane. I made for it, taking an extra turning or two in order to lose my pursuer. Coming to the big double doors, I slowed to a business-like stride, went in and demanded my car with a brisk tone, and bestowed a couple of notes on the attendant who brought her to me.

"Be coming back again?" he asked me cheerily.

"Oh, very likely," I lied, and because he was a blessedly human little man, I tipped him an extra pound, which made him goggle and stutter as he thanked me.

I shot the black car out into the street, turned left and lost myself in the maze of Manchester. The distant whistling of the searchers died out behind me.

Now, I thought, I was in the bloody soup. My description would be circulated in the other world, first of all. Well, I look like the common man, and that wouldn't help them much. Second, however, they'd be sure to discover that a fellow came into a garage in the vicinity and took his two-seater at the very rime the bobbies were hunting the Manchester Slasher (as the papers called me) thereabouts. That's elementary police work. So up to there all I really had to fret over was the ordinary human bloodhound business.

I'd given the garage a false name, naturally, when I took the old girl in to leave her. A purely automatic precaution. Lucky I have a turn for the criminal life, said I to myself smugly. Nothing to identify her with me, Will Chester of London.

Then there was my gear in the hotel.

Whoa! I slapped the wheel with one palm. I'd given the hotel the same fake name—Robert Hood—but in my Gladstone were half a dozen items with my own label on them. I'd intended a quick baggageless dash out of the city, before they traced me to the garage and sent out a call for a black Jaguar; but to leave without that damning luggage would be to present my true identity to the police in a matter of a few days, or even less. I headed for the hotel. Minutes counted, but so did that accursed Gladstone bag.

Then I bethought myself of the garage again. Of course they knew where I had been staying! That meant that within two minutes of the police—*they*—arriving at the garage and discovering that I had come in and hared out, the hotel would be receiving a call about me.

I groaned aloud. The Jaguar, sensitive to my thought waves or perhaps to the unconscious pressure of my foot, pounced forward at a law-shattering speed. Minutes counted? Seconds!

The hotel was no fly-by-night, tuppenny-ha 'penny wee place, for I had seen no reason on earth why I should not be comfortable while on my crusade; I put the Jaguar alongside the curb within a dozen paces of the entrance, walked nonchalantly in and demanded my key. The desk clerk was listening to the telephone. "One moment," he said, and then to me, holding his hand over the mouthpiece, "I think this is for you, sir."

MY mind speeded up and raced like a mad thing. No one would be calling me, so it must be *about* me; therefore the police had already found the garage; and the clerk must only have heard them say my name (my false name) within the instant. I imagined that they had said, "Have you a Mister Robert Hood staying there?" or something of the sort. Now I had two choices: I could bolt at once, leave my luggage to be inspected, and subsequently have my face plastered on every newspaper in England as the Manchester Slasher; or I could brazen it out. Instinctively I chose the right course, the only course. I bluffed to the top of my bent.

"Give me my key first," I said. He did so. "Now just tell 'em I'm not in, and hang up. It's a bloke I don't care to talk to."

"Ah," said he, smirking, "I see." To the instrument he murmured, "I'm sorry, Mister Hood is out at present," and— my eternal gratitude to that sleek-haired, smug-faced desk clerk!—rang off without asking if there was any message. He had given me a good half-minute of free time. I went to the lift and said, "Four please." If it had not been there I should have had to take the steps. Surely my luck was running that night!

I judged that, just about the time I struck the fourth floor, that phone at the desk would be sounding impatiently again. I opened my door, bolted it behind me, and began to throw things into my Gladstone.

My phone started to ring.

I emptied the drawers of the highboy, the devilish jangle in my ears; leaped into the bathroom and brushed my shaving kit and toilet articles into a little leather bag I used for them. I would be certain I was leaving nothing behind on which there might be a monogram, an engraved name...

Fingerprints! Great merciful God! I was packed. Everything I had brought with me was in the Gladstone.

The phone stopped ringing.

They would be on their way. A hotel detective or a couple of policemen, called in after that urgent message from the garage. Perhaps the usurpers—

I whipped out my handkerchief, wrapped it round my right hand, and started in to dust that room as no chambermaid had ever dusted it in all its memory. Each piece of wood that I might have touched in the past week received a quick vigorous swipe. Each glass and porcelain surface in the bathroom. Everything. The door knob. The glasses. Is that all? The window, which I'd raised a few times. Is that all? It that *all?*

I believed it was. I snatched up the Gladstone and with the cloth still around my hand I opened the door and slipped into the corridor.

Close the door, son. That'll halt them for a precious two seconds.

Down the corridor, around the first turn...

Safe, for the moment, safe!

And now what? Here was a flight of stairs. And in the distance I heard a lift door open.

Down the stairs I rushed, and was on the third floor.

Running for another flight, a different one, with a vague thought of confusing my trail, I stumbled and almost fell. Recovering, I fled down these, on down, down, down.

I was on the ground floor at last. The men's bar lay before me. The lobby was far away in the front of the building.

I straightened my tie, tried to appear like an eccentric who always carried a large brown bag with him, and paced into the bar.

As I put my hand—still swathed in the linen—to the outer door; the barman cried out, "'Ere, sir!" but I was gone. They would think I was an absconding guest. They would pursue me. But I shouldn't run, didn't dare run, along this street where humans and aliens strolled singly and in couples. I walked as fast as I thought I could without attracting attention. The hue and cry arose behind me. I came to the corner, rounded it without halting, and saw my dear old Jaguar twenty yards off.

I ran then, for there was no help, indeed there was deadly peril, in walking any longer. I went with great bounds, brushing aside people and *them* indiscriminately. Hurling the bag onto the seat, I hurdled it with a last burst of energy, crashed in behind the wheel, and in a flash my motor and I had leaped forward and were on our merry way.

We had gone a dozen blocks before I took my right hand off the wheel and unwrapped the handkerchief from it, stowing it away in the side pocket that also contained my hotel key. Mentally I checked over every clue to my true identity; so far as I could think, I had wiped them all out. Now all that remained was to get out of Manchester safely.

CHOOSING the darkest streets almost without volition, I had put a couple of miles between me and that by-now-surely-tumultuous deathtrap of a hostelry. I thought of roadblocks. One is always reading in American mystery stories of road blocks set up to catch thieves and murderers, but I had no notion as to whether they were used in England. Relying on the thought that at any rate I had never heard of one here, I tore for the outskirts of the city.

They would be on my trail. I kept seeing mental pictures of the alien beasts, sniffing me out like so many obscene bloodhounds. My hands grew slippery on the wheel with the sweat of fear. Then I put my panic behind me; *they*, after all would be working in the usual human channels, for surely they had at worst no more than a hazy suspicion that I could see them. True, I had relegated quite a few of them. But it must seem more likely to them that I was a maniac with luck on his side, rather than a seer. I doubted strongly that they would make such a concentrated effort at finding me as they had done last year with poor Jerry Wolfe. So I had only the laws and power of Old England to worry about.

Going over the past hour again and again, while driving, now at breakneck speed through deserted streets and now at a snail's pace in traffic, I decided that once I had left the city I had a very good chance of escaping entirely. Therefore I set myself to leave it as soon as possible. Beneath me the Jaguar purred contentedly as my foot caressed her accelerator.

And so the notorious Manchester Slasher went into the fastnesses of the Peak District, and laid his course south for Birmingham.

CHAPTER TEN

I did not take the Jaguar into Birmingham proper; I put her into a half-smashed, bombed-out old building I found quite by chance some few miles out of the city, and prayed that she would wait there for me till my business was done. It was then about four-thirty in the morning.

At a little tea-and-biscuit place in the suburbs I had a hearty breakfast, and read in an early edition the terrifying tale of the Manchester Horrors. It seemed that the infamous Slasher had been tentatively identified when he was tracked by the police to his lair in a well-known hotel; he was thought to be either a certain Irish communist agitator, or else a celebrated American gangster who I happened to know had been killed in 1937...

I walked on down to Birmingham and took a room in an obscure house in a slum district, run by a blowzy slattern who answered to "Old Mag." The parlor was equipped with a weary wireless set and an assortment of highly flavored gentlemen in the last stages of disrepair. One of them looked like a racetrack tout fallen on evil days, another I could have sworn was a professional mugger. A fitting den for the Manchester Slasher!

I was careful not to touch anything at all until I had gone out and bought a pair of thin silk gloves, which I wore at all times thereafter. The proprietor of the pawnship gave me a knowing wink as he handed them to me. I'm sure he thought I was a cat burglar or a safecracker. No one in my new home deigned to notice them. I must mention that, quite by accident and not through any searching on my part, I had happened to strike a place where none of the other-world brutes lived; I had been prepared to see a number of them here, but only found the lowly humans I have spoken of.

I spent my first evening in going over my clothing and other possessions, ripping out nametags, obliterating initials, and cleaning off fingerprints. I would not be trapped again as I had nearly been in Manchester.

THE second day and the early evening thereof I walked through the streets, thinking furiously. And the only conclusions I could come to anent my problems were bitter and lonely and hopeless.

Going "home" about eight o'clock, I wandered into the parlor and was accosted diffidently by a very low-looking form of life, which begged the pleasure of my company in a nearby hooch hut. I agreed. I would have stood drinks to a wolverine if the creature would have listened to me. I was starved for speech.

When I had bought him a few rounds, his taste running to that noble old British concoction, a four-o'-gin-hot, we began to talk freely: of anything, the weather, the latest race results, the difficulty of getting "real prime raw gin"…

He was a curious fellow. The name he gave me was Arold Smiff, which I imagine had once been Harold Smith; he was small and stringy and of a tobacco-brown hue, with eyes in which liquor-broken veins had long since stained the irises and the white to an all-over muddy crimson. He stank like a shebeen, his breath would have shriveled a brass monkey, but I soon noticed something really odd about him—he did not seem to be at all intoxicated. I made bold to comment on this.

"Why, General," he said, grinning wryly, "fak is, I been lushed for so long, I can't get lushed any more hardly at all. You ever had the snykes?"

I shook my head. He nodded wisely. "Ar, I thought not. You're clarss. Me, I got a permanent case of 'em, bloody snykes and 'orrors all the tyme. You wouldn't know what it's lyke, General, seeing such 'orrors all the bloody damn tyme."

Would I not, I said to myself, oh, would I not!

"No, you're clarss, any bloody fool could see that." He leaned over confidentially, and I could fairly feel my eyebrows curl under that breath. "Between pals, now, wot's your lay?"

"Lay?" I repeated idiotically.

"Gyme, General, gyme! I knew you was hot stuff the mo' I seen yer at Old Mag's. Wot's your specialty—jools?"

Good Lord! The man took me for a jewel-thief!

"Not exactly," I said.

WE were sitting in a booth. He craned his neck around to see that no one could overhear us. "Aye, but it's something fust-rate. You're no bloomin' snaveler nor knuckler."

"Ah, no," I agreed, presuming that, whatever they were, I couldn't be one of them.

"You're clarss," he repeated obstinately. "Me, I may not look so likely now, but once I was Manny Jarman's right'and lad."

I tried to look impressed, and wondered who Manny Jarman had been. A great deal of ale had flowed down my gullet at a good clip, and I was feeling reckless and friendly. "I'll tell you one thing," I said, "the police want me rather badly. I wouldn't tell you that if I didn't trust you."

"Ar! You trust Arold Smiff, General. 'E won't letcher down. I knowed you was on the lam when you come into Old Mag's. You're okay there. And you're okay so long as I'm your chum, too, see? I got connections." He brooded darkly over his connections. "Mugs, but they respecks old Arold Smiff, knowing wot 'e was once. Before the gin got 'im," he added significantly, peering into the depths of his glass. I snapped my fingers for another four-o'-gin-hot.

He chattered on, in his strange drunk-sober style, for a few minutes; and then, someone pushing by me, I moved my elbow to make more room in the aisle. In doing so I glanced up. It was one of *them*. A truly fearsome beast, this one: purplish, slimy and grotesque.

Arold bent closer, again singeing my eyebrows. "I'll give yer an example," he hissed. "Example o' wot I go through nowadyes. You seen that bloke leave?"

"Yes?"

"'E were a bloke to you, huh? Regular normal bloke?"

"Mmmm," I said noncommittally.

"Welp, me, I didn't see no bloke at all, d'yer get me? I seen a great big glob o' goop! A great big purple wet-looking barstid of a garstly freak! You think a joker's bad off when 'e's got snykes, huh? Wot about me, wot sees Frank and Stein's monsters all about?" He sat back triumphantly.

I suppose I gaped. I suppose my jaw dropped, my hands shook, my face grew pale. I don't know. For the moment the gin palace was a blur and my faculties were frozen, as Arold Smiff's words rang in my head.

Frankenstein monsters! Purple freak!

Fate had given me an ally worth more than all six of my band combined. A souse of an ally, a lowbred criminal of an ally, a gin-soaked worthless-appearing ally; but one who could see the aliens, evidently as plainly as I could myself!

Our gallant pioneer, Jerry Wolfe, had speculated that perhaps some people could see them when having a fit of what we call the D.T.'s—when they were saturated with alcohol, their vision was warped into the uncanny dimension-piercing angles which the musket blast had given me. Here was living proof of the theory. And here likewise was a fellow so permanently full of liquor (I swear the stuff ran in his veins) that he could see them *all the time!*

CHAPTER ELEVEN

"WHERE can we talk?" I asked him quietly, when I had got control of myself.

"Why, 'ere, General."

"No, no. A good safe place where we can talk privately and without interruption."

"Ow! Old Mag's, o' course. None better. Your room or mine."

"Mine," I said. "Let's go, old horse."

We went, taking along a bottle of gin for medicinal purposes. I sat him down in the dilapidated rocking chair, in my bedroom and, staring into his brown face intently, said, "I've got a proposition for you, Arold. It's a whopper, too."

"Big job?" he said. "You want me on a big job?"

"Yes, you. You'll be my partner in it."

"Me?" he repeated incredulously.

"You're the one chap who can help me."

The muddy eyes actually filled with tears; it was not a maudlin drunk's easy weeping, though, but the honest emotion of a humble workman who finds himself asked to assist a master. "You want me, Arold Smiff, to link up wiff you, a gent, a real gent, clarss, wot I mean a toff as ever was? Cor! I knowed I wasn't through yet," said he. "Just you lead on, General."

"I was only a Captain," said I.

"Then you didn't 'ave your deserts, I'll say. Wot's the gyme?"

"The biggest."

"Bank o' England?" he asked without much astonishment.

"No, not theft. We don't have to steal anything in this game."

He frowned, "'Old on, now, you mean I gotta knock somebody off? Scrag 'em?"

"Not you personally, Arold. You'll be too high in the game for that."

"Ow, not that I objecks, mindjer," he hastened to assure me. "It just took me off guard; as you might say, you not lookin' lyke a basher." He grinned. "'Twouldn't be the first mug I've did in, General."

"I'll wager on that," said I under my breath, and aloud, "I told you: you'll be too important in this affair to do any murdering yourself, Arold." I prodded him in the chest with a finger. "You'll give the orders," said I.

He was deeply impressed by that. "Cripes!" he said. "Me?"

"Yes. Now listen closely, and I'll, explain the whole business. Think back. Remember that purple monster you saw leaving the pub?"

"Not 'arf. Holy hell, not 'arf!"

"IT was something like a lizard in shape," I said slowly. "It had a long trailing tail, and two big hind legs it walked on; it had two sets of little forearms, only they weren't like arms, but more like big snakes: no fingers, no hands, just oozy rounded arms. It looked as if it had just crawled out of the sea, and around it there were a lot of thin silvery-blue lines, running at a tangent like this—" I chopped my hands through the air at a forty-five degree angle—"that seemed like a background to the creature. There were glowing eyes in its chest, and for a head it had what looked like a dead fish. Right?"

"Right." He gave me a long blank stare. Then he batted his lids up and down. "'Ow did you know? I never told you all that!"

"I saw it too."

"Garn!" he said scornfully. "Wotcher givin' us?"

"If I didn't see it, then how did I know just what it looked like?"

He thought that over, sucking his yellow teeth. Then he gasped. "My Gawd! You got 'em too?"

"Do I look drunk?"

"No, but—"

"And if I were, would I have seen exactly what you saw, unless it were really there?"

Arold Smiff sank back in the rocker and let out a wheeze that began in the tips of his toes. "My old mother! I'm off it for good. The snykes are catchin'. Ow! *'O are you, mister?"*

I threw my whole hand into the center of the table, staking everything on it.

"I'm the Manchester Slasher," I said.

He recoiled. His brown face, incapable of turning pale, nonetheless gave the effect of blanching in some mysterious manner of its own. The common little thief and garden-variety mugger quailed before the celebrated Mad Ghoul of Manchester. He drew out a large clasp knife and snapped open the blade, his hand shaking. "'Ere, now, you keep back from me, you 'ear? I'm not to be trifled wiff, see? You touch me and you're a deader, that's wot."

"Oh, put it away," I said fiercely. When he refused, I grabbed his wrist with my left hand and struck it a stinging judo blow with my right; the knife fell.

"Ow-er!" he yelled. "You keep back!" Cowering, he gazed at me with those muddy crimson eyes wide, his mouth stretched in a nervous, sickly grimace of fear. "Twenty you done in, all in a couple of dyes," he whispered. "And I been and gone and drunk wiff you lyke you was my brother. You're mad-dorg crazy, you are."

"I'M as sane as you are," I said, "or saner. For heaven's sake, man, get hold of yourself. Do you think I stood you a bucket of gin and wasted two hours on you just to murder you in my own room?"

"Welp, no," he said grudgingly.

"Up north I killed four in the time I've taken to talk to you," I said, to impress him further. "Now listen closely, because I don't want to go over this more than a couple of times. In the first place, those people I killed weren't people."

"Garn!"

"They were beasts like the purple lizard. Some of 'em were worse. I killed one that was like a giant hoptoad with fangs."

"I've seen 'em like that... 'Ere, wotcher giving us? *I* know them 'orrors is all in my mind. *I* ain't no common lushington. *I* knows it's the gin. *I* know they're folks like everyone."

"Oh, *you* know, do you? Open up that walnut you call your mind, chum. Why do we both see the identical brutes, if they're in your mind?"

"I dunno," he growled sullenly.

"Then just sit quiet—there's the gin beside you—and I'll explain it all in words of one syllable."

And this I did. I went over the whole frightful business, with a side dissertation on the theory of a fourth dimension. Then I went over it again. Somewhere in the distance a clock struck two. I summarized it again. I could see it beginning to penetrate to his submerged intellect. I went through it all a fourth time, and his murky gaze began to glow. The faraway clock struck three.

"'Ere," he said at last. "You ain't loony at all, are yer? Tell me agayn about them as is in it wiff yer."

"There's an old Colonel, a real big gun in his day, with pots of money. There's two veterans, gentlemen both, and one the son of a lord. There's a doctor with plenty of brains, and an old chap with more dignity than you ever saw in your misspent life. There's even a girl, a real lady. And there's me. Do you think we'd all be chucking our lives into this mess if we didn't know it was desperately real?"

HE scratched his nose with a black nail. "No," he said, "no, you wouldn't. I can see as you're real clarss, ripper or no. What d'yer want of me, though? I'm plain dirt compared wiff you."

"Why, you were Manny Jarman's right-hand man," I said. "You haven't forgotten what it's like to be top dog?"

He was immensely flattered at that. "Thank you kindly, General. You sees deeper into a bloke than most. Go on."

"I've only a hazy idea of what I want you to do, Arold, when the time comes. But here's an important part of it. Could you find me a whole raft of fellows who'd be willing to commit murder for money, no questions asked?"

"Hell," he grinned, "could a cat find garbage cans?"

"They'd have to be given definite instructions, and be the kind of men who would carry them out to the letter. And no copper's narks, see? Nobody who'd take our cash and then squeal."

"I could do it," he said, thinking. "I could get bullies 'ere in Brummagem who'd cut their mothers' necks for three quid. And they could get others. Ow, trust Arold Smiff to find the right 'uns!"

"We might need a hundred."

"There's that many and more."

I was giving slow birth to a real plan now. "It might be that they'd have to go all over England, and do these murders in a hundred different places. And they'd have to do them in a certain manner you'd tell 'em about, see? No slipshod hatchet work, but well-planned assassinations."

"Might be harder to find them as would work precise to orders, but I could do it. I know every rogue in these parts, don'tcher doubt it, General."

"That's why you're so valuable, Arold; that's why you'll be *my* right-hand man. And only you and I must know that the men we'll be killing aren't truly men, but—"

"But oosluppers," agreed Arold, proud of the new word. "Oosluppers from the fourth demented, yus. Why, General, it's lyke a crusade, a bloody noble crusade, ain't it?"

"That's what we think, pal. But that part's a deep secret."

"Hot knives won't drag it outen me," he bragged. "Gawd, to think I been seein' these 'ere Frank and Stein's monsters for eight years more or less, and thought all the time it was the gin!" He made his apologies to the liquor by taking an enormous gulp of it.

"Now I've got to go away for a while, Arold," I told him. "I've got to travel all over this island, and collect some names. When I've done that I'll let you know. Meanwhile you can be lining up your lieutenants. With care, old horse, with the greatest care." Then it occurred to me that he had never asked what his reward would be. "You'll find yourself a rich man when this is over, Arold."

"Garn, what'd I do wiff a lot o' money? I don't need much but gin and a few comforts now and agayn, and maybe a bit o' cash to swank it wiff, around town."

"You'll be able to build a swimming pool and fill it with Gordon's if you do your job right."

"Trust old Arold, General."

"I do," I said. "I do."

"That's damn near thanks enough," said he in a choked voice. There was a stratum of pretty fine stuff in Arold

Smiff, besides the streak of sentimentality you'll usually find in your lower-class Briton.

"Now," I went on, "here's the plan. I'll go over it until we both know it word for word."

I sketched it out as it had come to me in this strange night of lengthy explanation. Then I repeated it, and re-repeated it, until I thought it would bubble out of our ears.

And when the clock rang five, we were nearly ready to begin. But first we laid ourselves down to sleep for a few hours, till the pubs had opened again; when we arose, and put on our coats, and sallied out together to commit a murder…a most unpleasant but most necessary murder.

CHAPTER TWELVE

I walked out of Birmingham alone, just before noon, heading for the bombed-out old building in which I had left the Jaguar, with my Gladstone bag locked in her dickey, or rumble seat. I had not carried any baggage with me into the city except my razor, toothbrush, knife and automatic, and my pipe.

It occurs to me that, since she played nearly as useful a part in my adventures as did my human colleagues, I should perhaps devote a moment to describing my black Jaguar. I had bought her late in 1937 for a matter of some four hundred pounds, and except for the war years, which she waited out in a barn near my home in Coventry, we had been inseparable ever since. She was one of the mighty Standard Swallow 100's, with a wonderfully reliable three-and-a-half-liter engine, and as I've said, I once clocked her at a hundred and fourteen m.p.h. and believed she could do more. She would go from a standstill to eighty m.p.h. in a matter of twenty-seconds, for her acceleration was ferocious. Yet she was the smoothest-riding jade I ever owned. Her brown leather upholstery had faded through the years to a rich old tan, but her heart was as young as ever. I had lavished on her the affection that might more properly have gone to a wife or a kennel of hounds; in my lonely careering about the countryside in these last days she had amply repaid me. She had been companion and steed and confidante to a very homesick man.

It was a clear day, with a promise of sultry heat to come that prickled my body with sweat under the old tweed suit. I tramped briskly along, thinking of Marion—I thought of her whenever I could, for her sweet face shut out the menacing usurpers from my mind—until I came in sight of the wrecked building. As I swung down the hill toward it, I heard voices raised in argument.

CAUTIOUSLY I slowed a little, looking nonchalant and disinterested. I walked past the ruin and from the corner of my eye saw a number of men (and monsters) clustered around the Jaguar looking at her curiously. "Aye," said one of them, "that's his, right enough. Black Jaggiar, it says here on the prints." Two of them were constables. I ambled over.

Now this was a particularly idiotic thing to do, but I must plead extenuating circumstances. In the first place, I had just been a partner in the commission of a messy homicide, and was strung up as high as a barrage balloon. Secondly, I had been hardheaded and coldly practical for many hours— indeed, since the night of my last murder in Manchester I had not done an impetuous act, nor played the swaggering gam- bler with death for any stakes except the highest. It suddenly came to me that I must do a doughty deed, act the bold Quixote for once, to liven up my interest and tone up my reflexes. I was never born to be an ice-brained plotter, although I had been forced by fate into that uncongenial role. Rather for me the swirling cape and impetuous rapier, the big-plumed hat and gallant gesture, the fiery and slightly ridiculous *beau geste*. So I ambled into the wrecked building.

The men (and monsters) turned to stare at me. I could see the great brutes of aliens turning orange and green with interest. I had learned that they often swelled and changed color when intrigued or alarmed. "Cheero," I said vacuously. "What's up?"

One of the group, a portly constable with a red face, eyed me dourly and said, "Stranger 'ereabouts, sir?"

"I'm on a walking tour," said I. "Just spent a night in Birming'm. Saw you chaps in a rum sweat over something, thought I'd have a dekko. Dashed sleek-lookin' car, what?"

"Ar," said the constable, observing my boots. They were stout and old, the very thing for a walking tour. "You know anything about motors, sir?"

"Me? Lord, no," said I. I then giggled, which pained him visibly. "I wouldn't touch one. Cousin owned one, name of Algy; cousin, you know, not the car. Turned over in a treacherous manner and simply squashed him like a bloomin' bug. What's up with this one?"

THE monsters were scrutinizing me intently. I told myself that I needn't be afraid of their inspection: in addition to my quite ordinary features, which could scarcely have been described in much detail by their compatriot who had seen me, I was at the moment wearing the shell-rimmed spectacles which I ordinarily used only for reading, being far-sighted as an eagle. I had put them on a few moments before, just in case.

An alien said, leaning his human form toward me, "We think it may be the Manchester Slasher's."

If he thought to startle me into betraying myself, he was disappointed. I fluttered my hands and bleated. "Gad! Not that murderer chappie? The one who killed about ninety people up north?"

"Twenty, sir." The alien appeared to relax. "Yes, it fits the description, all right." He turned to another. "Tom, you'd best go and telegraph Manchester. Sam, you go with him and bring back another couple o' boys. We'll just lay us a trap."

I walked all about the Jaguar, prodding her bonnet and peering at the dashboard gingerly. "Deuced mysterious affairs, motors," I said. "Don't see how anyone can tell what gadget to push next."

"We're a-going to lay an ambush for this 'ere Slasher, sir, if you don't mind," said one of them.

"Hear hear," I said. "Chop the blighter, what? Pip him in the early counties, right?"

"There's liable to be trouble, sir," insinuated another.

"Rather," I yammered. "Oh, rather."

"We'd like to get ready now, *if* you please, sir."

"Oh, absolutely. Carry on. Lay a snare for the wretched person, lads," said I heartily.

"You'd better leave now, sir," said the constable firmly. "Before there's trouble, you know. Wouldn't want to get hurt."

"Heavens, no," said I. "I say, officer, could I just sit in that seat a mo'? Give one something to boast of, what?"

"No, sir. There may be fingerprints in the thing."

"I WON'T touch a bally thing," I assured him, and as there was no one within six feet of me, I hopped in behind the wheel. At once they all shouted angrily; but there was no suspicion of me yet. It is the firm belief of the lower-middle classes that anyone who bleats and says "bally" and "dashed" is a regular Bertie Wooster character and as harmless as a sheep, although somewhat less attractive. "Come out o' that, sir!" yelled the constable.

"Just want to get the feel of it, you know," said I reassuringly. "Want to tell old Algy I sat in what's-his-name's seat."

"I thought you said Algy was killed in a wreck."

"That was Algy Witherspoon, my cousin," I told him reproachfully, secretly extracting the ignition key from my pocket. "This is young Algy Pope, my *other* cousin. Regular ripping chappy on murders and all that, Algy is. Tell you all about Crippen, and whoozis that did in his maiden aunt over at that little place in Sussex, and all such bloody—pardon the expression—goin's-on. Likes birds, too. Sits about in swamps watchin' them. Deuced rum feller."

Suspicion must have dawned just about then. *They* moved toward me, while the humans still hesitated. I slid the key in under cover of my bent body, chortling something inane about the mythical Algy, and stepped on the clutch. A hand was laid heavily on my shoulder. The Jaguar leaped backwards at the same instant, hit someone who reeled away with a scream, rocked crazily over the rubble and struck the road. I twisted her madly around, waved my hand in a cavalier-like manner, and sped off southeastward on the great road that leads to London. Shouts of rage followed me. I patted the Jaguar's wheel. "Everything's all right, baby," I said. "Old Will is back. It'll all be all right now."

I devoutly hoped that it would be.

CHAPTER THIRTEEN

IT is a hundred and fifteen or twenty miles from Birmingham to London. Having gambled the fate of the world on a silly trick, and won back my two-seater from the very hands of the law and of the usurpers, I was wonderfully buoyed up; and decided to go down to my gang's headquarters and tell them all the new developments. I was aching to talk to someone...preferably Marion.

In half an hour I had left Birmingham and then Coventry far behind me, and was feeling pretty safe, as there had been no signs of pursuit. Then, just as I roared into some cursed little hamlet along the route—I don't even know its name—a great black motor dashed out of a lane ahead of me and blocked the way. I saw it was crammed to the roof with *them;* knew that this was no accidental barrier, but a contingent of the enemy, either lawful or of the misbegotten underground of the beasts; and without pausing ran the Jaguar up over the curb, squeezed through between their car and the wall of a shop, rocketed on two wheels back into the road and trod the accelerator down to the floor. The black job was after me in a flash. We howled through that hamlet like a pair of greased lightning bolts.

They gave me only a few bad minutes; when we hit the open road I drew away as though—to coin a stunning simile—they had been standing still. But even when their dust was no more than a puff on the horizon, I gnawed my lips and worried. My course was known, and the telegraphs and telephones would be crackling far in advance of me. Yet doggedly, and perhaps rather stupidly, I held to this main road until I had come nearly to St. Albans, for I could eat up the miles so swiftly on decent paving that it gave me the illusion of outrunning my enemies. At last, just before the old cathedral town, I turned off and lost myself in the network of country byways.

EVENING was closing in when at last I rolled the black lass to a halt at a garage in the south of London. The owner was an old mate of mine with whom I'd seen a lot of action in the war. What lies I told him don't matter: suffice it that in three minutes the Jaguar was stowed in a dark corner of his big shed, and he had contracted to paint her a deep red hue by next afternoon…and to keep quiet about her. Gladstone in hand, I then set out for The Gray Gander. I told myself that (a) I would be less conspicuous there than at the toney Gloucester Club or the exclusive Albany, (b) although three of my men were billeted at the latter place, Alec Talbot was the most able of the whole band, despite his single arm, and he was at the inn, (c) I did not want to be seen by any of the aliens who knew me—I hardly realized why, but I had the creepy feeling that *they* would somehow penetrate my secret—and on the single occasion when I had visited the Gander, I had seen none of the beast-folk. Finally I admitted to myself that these reasons were so much rot, and actually (d) Marion Black was drawing me like an irresistible whirlpool draws a chip of flotsam.

I went up to Alec's room, closed the door behind me, and fell on his bosom. He beat me on the back and gurgled wordlessly. I beat him on the back and sputtered idiotically. It was a grand reunion.

"Where's Marion?" I asked.

"I'll get her." He dashed out and brought her back. When she came into the room, lighting it up like a sunburst in a cavern, I took her in my arms and kissed her long and well.

"Marion, will you marry a poor devil who loves you in a humble but most passionate manner?"

"After one kiss?" asked Alec blankly. "Just *one* kiss?"

"Certainly," she said. "That can be remedied."

"Oh, Lord, not immediately," groaned Alec, as we began to do so. "Let him tell us where in hell he's been for seventeen years. Let him relieve my mind."

I ended the second kiss with a splutter. "Good God! I can't ask you to marry me, dearest. I—come and sit down— I'm a murderer."

"You can't call it murder, son, to chop an inhuman monster," said Alec.

"But I'm wanted by every policeman in the Kingdom. You see, I'm the Manchester Slasher."

I DON'T know what reaction I expected of Marion...the pale cheek, the indrawn gasp, the expression of loathing and fear...as a matter of fact, she clapped her hands and laughed.

"You owe Geoff ten bob, Alec!" she cried.

"Huh?" said I.

"Geoff bet Alec ten shillings that you were the Mad Ghoul. He said—"she became serious—"he said that one just couldn't give a man the power to see such nightmares as you've been seeing, and expect him to keep a cool head and not strike at them. He said he had wild bursts of fury himself when he thought of *them*, and knew if he could see them, he'd start a reign of terror."

"I thought you'd draw back with abhorrence," I said.

She threw her arms around me. "Oh, Will, poor old Will! My Uncle Geordie was a big game hunter, and I think he was a much more reprehensible character than you. After all, darling, the beasts you're stalking are far worse than any innocent old family-man of a lion."

"Say," put in Alec, "something's been puzzling me. Why haven't the coppers spotted the license of your Jaguar? It's famous, you know—on the wireless every hour these days."

"Oh, my dear chap! I stole a set of plates off a big Daimler before I ever left London. You're dealin' with a hardened crook." I told them how I had rescued her from the hands of the enemy in Birmingham. "It was the serial numbers on her innards that worried me. Except for them, though, she couldn't be traced to me." I kissed my girl again. Her lips were like a drug that drew me back again and again for larger doses.

Alec clucked his tongue. "Most unEnglish!"

"See here, chum: you trot out and collect the lads. Have 'em come here unobtrusively by ones and twos, and we'll have a council of war."

"Oh, all right, if you don't want an appreciative audience to make funny remarks at appropriate places." He slapped on his hat and went out, while I returned to Marion's embrace. For a little while I could forget the whole abominable race of beast-people, the dire venture before me, and everything else except the incredible fact that she returned what I had always considered my hopeless love.

CHAPTER FOURTEEN

IT was grand to see my half-dozen sub rosa crusaders gathered together again, sitting expectantly on sofas and chairs in Alec's room, watching me with friendship and love. What a tonic those comradely faces were! I drank a silent, sentimental toast to them, and began my yarn.

First I told them of Arold Smiff, the cheap, crooked, gin-soaked little man, who had taken his last bath in 1922; the man who could see the usurpers as well as I could. That roused them to gleeful vociferance, which I squashed with a bark. "Quiet, will you! I'm half starved—haven't had a bite since breakfast. I want to get this done, so I can go and eat a good dinner.

"You know that when I left you I could see just one dismal possibility—a long campaign or slaughter, slaughter, slaughter. But when I met Arold, a plan grew up in my mind—"

"Like a lovely flower in a swamp," murmured Geoff, "Sorry. Pray continue."

"The whole plan," I growled, "is about nine-tenths sheer bluff; but I think it may work. Here it is: first, I travel around the country and collect a hundred names; the names of usurpers whose human shells have had more or less spectacular careers. Not those born to the purple, but those who've come up like rockets, self-made men who've climbed to posts of importance in politics, the law, and elsewhere. I've seen a number of big shots of that sort who are nothing really but robots moved by slimy misshapen blobs...and I've deduced (pardon the Holmesian expression) that the important members of their loathsome breed are probably those who rise to take over important positions in this world. That allows 'em to protect and to advance their secret cause."

"How?"

"By passing certain laws, and—well, here's an example. One of them commits some crime, perhaps inadvertently. *They* don't want him to get chucked into prison, where he'd be no use to them in furthering the birth-rate. So a were-policeman, to coin a name, will let him escape; or a were-judge will set him free. Get the poisonous subtlety of it? They work themselves into posts where they can help each other to the top of their bent. Even on the lower levels, they're often bartenders and hotelkeepers, who can pass quick word of developments, and so forth. It's as if a lot of Nazis had become lawyers and judges and M. P.'s here during the late fracas, and from their exalted seats had protected whole battalions of lesser spies when they ran afoul of the cops."

"I see," said the Colonel. "That's logic."

"SO it stands to reason that, if I want to put a great big crimp in their plans, I have to chop a slice off the top of their organization, rather than out of the bottom. I slew a score of 'em while I was the Manchester Slasher, but those were common low folk whom I can't see as especially important to the general plan of the usurpers. They got very peeved about me, but it was nothing to the way they'd have acted had I murdered twenty judicial were-people, or twenty husks of Members of Parliament. My score of twenty lower-case aliens might have been accidental, but twenty upper-crusters wouldn't be. And a hundred will make them sit up and scream like hell.

"You can't hire decent men to commit pointless assassinations, so of course I was handicapped until I met Arold Smiff. In fact, I never even thought of *hiring* killers, until that night when I found that he could see 'em too. Then the dawn flashed up. You *can* pay professional rogues to commit murders, and no questions asked. So I deputized Arold to go out and collect a hundred scoundrels for me: the most reliable riffraff available, men who would, as he says, do in their old mothers for a chew of tobacco. He's to pay them ten pounds apiece in advance, with a promise of ten more when the business is done. Then, on a certain night, and within a period of a few hours, they're to strike all over England—and slay these usurpers I'll have collected in my little black book. I understand that the underworld looks with disfavor on a gentleman who collects a fee from a brother crook and then doesn't deliver the goods, so I believe that most of these cutthroats will keep faith and comply with his instructions."

"How do you know, this Smith won't do a bunk with your money?" asked Doctor Baringer cynically. "After all, a common thief—"

"Not common," said I loyally. "He was Manny Jarman's right-hand man."

"Who in blazes is, or was, Manny Jarman?"

"Haven't the foggiest, John…anyhow, Arold's been promised a lot of cash if he comes through; he's enthralled with the scheme, for after all he's been seeing these pink and crimson cacodemons since the early '40's; lastly, and maybe most important, he knows I'm the Manchester Slasher, and in his heart of hearts he's scared white of me. I felt no qualms at all about giving him eleven hundred quid."

Alec whistled. "What a wad!"

"Nearly all I had with me. It's a lucky thing some of us are loaded with the ready, for this affair will cost like sin.

"Then, after our pogrom, I call one of *their* bigwigs and tell him to meet me somewhere, with as many of his pals as he wants to bring. I say to 'em, 'Gents, you've just seen a sample of my power. I've reached out and obliterated a hundred of you, and they weren't any small potatoes either, but some o' your finest. You realize I didn't snag 'em all by myself; you're no village idiots. Those killings were done by a hundred chaps who can *see* you. We struck at you all over England. In a few days, another hundred of you get it—and some of you here now are on that list. Couple days later, a hundred and fifty. Then two hundred. And we'll go on knocking you over regularly, working from the top down, till there aren't any of your breed left here, and damned good riddance to filthy bad rubbish, too.'

"THEN I make my point. 'The nub of the thing is this: we want you to go home. Pick up your kilts and vamoose. Beat it. This world isn't your world, and by heavens you'd better leave it while the leaving is good. Otherwise you're sunk. You can murder me now,' I tell 'em generously, 'but there's plenty more where I came from. We've perfected a system of warping our vision, and every day there are more of us who can see you in all your ugliness. You can't beat us, because we're the best underground organization that ever existed; and last night's massacre proves it. Till now you had no idea we even existed. Did you?' And they have to admit they didn't, because we don't."

"How's that again, Will?"

"Never mind. Anyway, then they think it over, and if we're in luck, they decide the hell with it, and go home."

"Leaving thousands of suddenly dead bodies, and incredible misery and sorrow among the friends of their puppets," said Geoff. "Oh, I'm with you. That's our whole objective, to rid ourselves of them. But it just hit me: what a lot of tears will be shed because we stepped into this matter."

"Shall we turn back now?"

"Don't drivel. Only...great merciful powers!" He drank from his glass, his hand shaking. "What will we wreak!"

"Do you think it'll work, Will?" asked Marion quietly.

"It's the biggest bluff of all time, darling. But it must work!" I paused. "There's one big factor. I've hinted at it— here it is. We've always taken it for granted that when the human body dies, the usurper simply goes back to his own world and begins again by getting himself born into a new husk here. Jerry Wolfe figured that out originally, and we've accepted his theory as gospel. But I submit that it needn't be true. I don't know why I ever thought it was. How do we know what happens to the monster when its hull of human flesh dies? How do we know that it's only the puppet that perishes? Echo answers: *we don't know*. Maybe the aliens are so bound to their false humans in this dimension that when the bodies die, the aliens must die too. What's so impossible about that? After all, I've told you that *they* haven't any powers here except those of the bodies they inhabit. God knows what they can do in their own never-never land—but here, they're little better than so many natural-born people. And if they're that restricted, that much identified with these puppets, maybe even their death is mutual."

I CLEARED my throat and took a drink of Scotch. "What happened when I killed my first ogre? I went to a pub with Geoff and watched. Pretty soon all the beasts sittin' there started to flap their arms at one another and turn different colors, and then a lot of them got up and left. Aha, yes, I said to myself, the gorgon who got his has gone around behind the dimension-screen telling his chums about it. But I was arguing from a false premise. I was basing my ideas on what I believed to be a fact—yet that fact hadn't been proven at all, and probably couldn't be proven this side of the silver land!"

"Nor disproven," put in Alec.

"But I can show you more to disprove it than you can dig up to prove it! What happens when I assassinate an alien? His human vehicle croaks, while he himself swells up, turns a vivid horrid hue, and goes pop. I submit that that looks more like the death of the alien itself than a simple relegation to another region.

"But I think *they* can leave this world voluntarily, in which case they go on living in their own. Lord knows how long a life expectancy they've got, over there. Maybe their time is different from ours, so that the life of a man occupies no more than a fraction of a day in the silver land; the theft of a body and the puppeteering of it from womb to tomb may be no more than an hour's vicious pastime for an alien."

"I've been thinking of that," said Geoff slowly. "I see this whole business as a kind of fierce joke on their part, the slow and sly winning of a world from its unseeing inhabitants. So perhaps they'll leave us if their lives are endangered—perhaps the joke may not be worth dying for."

"All this," interrupted John Baringer testily, "is off the track, and really no more than so much anthropomorphism. How can a man finally and definitely state *what* are the purposes of a pack of inhuman beings? Go on, Will."

"Well, to prove my new theory, Arold and I went out to a pub this morning. We chose a frightful creature that was doing some solitary drinking, and Arold, who's a whizzer of a lad at such matters, slipped some slow poison into his liquor.

"We watched him die, in the throes of agony, which was taken by all the other denizens of the pub for simple indigestion or appendicitis. It took him twelve minutes to die on the floor. I timed him.

"THE first three minutes he just writhed and changed colors and shot off angry sparks. He didn't know he was dying. I refer to the real entity, not the human part. Obviously he could feel the pain—they must be able to, otherwise they'd give themselves away by not making the human body jump when it's stuck with a pin, or sits on a hot stove, or whatnot—you can see that. Well, after those three minutes, he seemed to wake up to the fact that this was it. Immediately he started to leave this dimension. It was the damndest sight I ever laid eye on. It was like a man trying to haul himself out of quicksand or heavy muck. The beast wrenched upward, and jerked back, and did what in any normal being would be called shrugging his shoulders, for all the world as if he was mired in something and wanted to get out. He had an awful time of it. Took him seven minutes and fifteen seconds. But at last he made it.

"He oozed back and away from that twisting body on the floor. He stood there, weaving and trembling, and I'll bet he was sweating, too, if *they* do any such prosaic thing as sweat. He was entirely divorced from the husk—which lived, mind you, for more than a minute after he'd left it. But as soon as he'd stepped away, he began to fade; and within three or four seconds he had vanished. At any rate, from my sight, and Arold's."

I signaled to Alec to fill my glass. "That's why I think they die when I murder them; because of the time it took that critter to get loose from his puppet. He was scared. I could feel it, just as I can feel their ordinary waves of hatred and abominable passions. I could sense the terror that filled that usurping bastard when he knew his husk was dying. He was purely scared to hell! Why? Why, unless he knew he'd die in both worlds if he couldn't rid himself of the shell before it perished?"

I sighed. I was tired of this whole rotten business, and light-headed from the liquor on my empty stomach. I said, "It was what I'd wanted to discover, why we poisoned the thing. I'd recalled that every alien death I'd seen, every one Jerry Wolfe saw, had been sudden and quick. I'd realized that there were no data on slow deaths. I had to have some. I got it. And I say, it's two to one *they* die when the human part dies, unless they have plenty of time to get away from it. That's the reason I think they'll leave us voluntarily, in a terrific hurry, when they think there's a whole crew of seers after 'em. They don't like death any more than we do. Death's a queer, an uncanny thing. Nothing that I know in nature likes to die."

"But how did the aliens in those pubs of yours learn so quickly about the killings, if the one who was killed—I mean the one—" Marion frowned angrily—"if the one who'd been relegated didn't go around behind the scenes and tell them?"

"Oh, dear girl!" shouted Geoff. "Messengers! Errand boys! The pony express of the silver land!"

"That's it," said I. "That's what we never thought of. There must be plenty of *them* who don't have human bodies at all, and move freely in their own dimension. What's to keep them from spreading the word to their comrades when one dies?"

"Will, you've hit it," the Colonel said. "They die here. It's probable, it's the best news yet, and if it's true, the bluff will work."

"And now that I've lectured you for an hour," I said, reaching for Marion's hand, "let's go out to the best restaurant within walking distance, and have us a monstrous dinner. I could eat the proverbial horse."

"There's a place within two blocks where they give you a delightful Percheron steak," said Alec. "Let's travel."

CHAPTER FIFTEEN

WE ate a noble meal, sat long over the port, and came out into a deep July night canopied with a velvet turquoise sky in which the full moon was riding high. We began to stroll along, talking of inconsequential things; at the corner of Baker Street we split up, the others heading for their own digs, while Alec and Marion and I went toward the inn. As we passed beneath a lamp, I happened to glance over my shoulder. I do not know to this day whether I heard the footsteps, or sensed the hate-aura of the beast, or perhaps was warned by the primitive instincts that I had been developing through the past weeks of terror; whatever caused it, I peered back down the street, and saw one of the aliens following us. In the moonlight his human body was a dark form within an envelope of gray-blue mist.

Coincidence, I told myself, angry to feel the sweat leap out on my face and palms. Nonetheless, I had a second look in a moment, just as the thing was walking under the lamp. I was rewarded by a strange sight: in the flood of brilliant light I saw the puppet-body of the man all stark and clear and black, with the distorted form of the usurper about it flaming like a gaudy, transparent rainbow. It was an awesome spectacle, and sent the cauld grue racing up my backbone.

"Alec," I hissed from the corner of my mouth, "I'm going to stop in a minute. Take a good look at the bloke that's following us."

Then we halted, and to give us an excuse, I took out a cigarette and lit it. The monster passed us. I thought the moon-grayed protoplasm had a 'tinge of orange, which might indicate deep interest on the being's part, but I could not be sure. When it was out of hearing I said, "Anyone we know?"

"It's a man from the restaurant," said Marion. "I noticed him looking at us as we ate. I thought he was flirting with me."

"He gave you a damn hard stare, Will," said Alec.

"Jerusalem!" I growled. "May be a coincidence, but—he's one of *them*...and I let him have a ruddy good look at me with that match!"

"Could he have chased you from up north?"

"No, no. Nobody followed me on the roads I took, son. But he and his gang have my description." I threw away the cigarette angrily. "'Course, I look like anybody else, but—"

"You do not!" protested Marion. "You're very handsome, for one thing."

Alec laughed briefly. "Well, maybe not that, Will, but you are individual enough to be spotted from a good description."

I was astonished. I had never thought so. I said, "We've got to be careful, then. Can't let him see us go into The Gray Gander."

WE walked past our inn. The creature had disappeared. We went on a short distance, and then I felt from the prickling of the hair on my neck that he was behind us again.

So began a game of cat and mice; which took us around corners and fleeing through alleys until at last I felt we had lost our silent pursuer, and with a sigh we entered our tavern.

I was awakened next morning, as I slept uneasily on Alec's couch, by Doctor John Baringer. He was puffing a pipe and grinning, but his eyes were shadowed. "What's up?" I asked.

"Everybody but you... Will, there's a lashing of people about in Baker Street. I don't know why I noticed 'em, especially, but they're there—just standing or sauntering, watching folk pass. It struck me queerly, and Alec tells me you were followed last night."

I started to dress hurriedly. "Do they look like policemen?"

"I wouldn't say so," John mused. "They're just ordinary people, men and women both, standing in the sun. I can't say I like it."

"Nor I. Are they concentrated near the inn?"

"No. Within a block or two, though; I didn't begin to notice them till I'd passed that restaurant where we ate last night."

Alec came in, "You were right," he said to John. "By God, you were right! Forty or more, loitering... Will's got to get out."

"Will's got to lie low," snapped the physician. "They obviously don't know just which building he's hiding in. He'll have to stop here until the fiends give up."

"Or at least until I can slip out at night," I said. "I say! Does it occur to you that the blighters now have *all* our descriptions? We were under observation last night for an hour or two! Call—"

Alec was already pouncing on the phone. He rang through to the Albany, spoke ten words, and hung up with a long face. "The Colonel and Geoff are out. That means they're headed here. Too late! By the powers, we're dished!"

"Maybe not," I said hopefully. "It could be coincidence."

"And I could be the Lost Dauphin of France," said Alec gloomily. He put in a call to the Gloucester Club, got hold of Johnson, and told him to stay there till he heard from us. Then we waited, fretting, for Geoff and the Colonel: who came in blithely at ten.

WE sat there, staring at one another morbidly, and argued and plotted futilely through a dragging, hot hour or two. It was dreadfully hard to decide on a plan, for now it was not a question of getting me out of London, but of finding a haven for all of us.

"You've got to collect a hundred names, if you hope to put that affair of yours through," said Geoff, chewing his pipestem. "You can't do that sittin' here on your well-cushioned behind. Your chum Arold will be gathering his ragtag army in Brummagem, and you've got to be ready to use 'em. Look here! Why not we form a flying wedge and bust you out o' here right now? If they're not coppers—and they didn't smell like the law to me when we passed 'em—they won't stop six of us in broad daylight. Wouldn't dare. We'll take Alec's Rolls and ditch them. Then we'll split up out of London, and you can put on a false beard and go it alone, if you like, or with one of us as sidekick. How's that sound?"

"I don't want to leap into it with both feet," I said. "Let's wait it out a bit. Maybe there's nothing in it. Maybe those people simply like to loiter in Baker Street. Maybe they're tourists, watching for Watson and Holmes." Dismal worries about the safety of Marion and my friends were crowding my mind, preventing rumination.

So we argued until luncheon, which we ordered sent up to the room; after which John went out to reconnoiter. He was soon back.

"Still there! There's no mistake, they're watching for you, Will. I couldn't be sure, but they may have noticed me, too." He scowled. "I hope not...but they're clever as sin."

So, mainly because I was too unsure of myself to risk a bold move such as Geoff had suggested, we waited out the first half of the afternoon in the rooms of The Gray Gander. And nothing happened at all.

CHAPTER SIXTEEN

AT three o'clock or thereabouts, there was a knock at the door. We all "stared at each other with a wild surmise," and then Colonel Bedford resolutely flung it open. I was sitting on a footstool beside Marion's chair, in such a position that I could not see the stranger; who said in an oily, semi-cultured tone, "Good day, sir! I'm making a survey—"

"Step in," said our old soldier. "Step right in, sir."

"Oh, no, I shan't bother you now, as I see you're having a bit of a gathering," said the unctuous voice. "I'll call round la—"

At this point the Colonel took him firmly by the lapels of his coat. Alec said afterwards that he never saw astonishment spread over a face so quickly. The man's mouth remained open in the middle of the word. The Colonel, a man of action who had been bottled up too long, now picked up our caller and genially hurled him halfway across the room. He slammed the door and turned the key, took it out of the lock and pocketed it with a sinister grin. Then he, as well as most of the other lads, gave me a brief inquiring glance. I nodded. It was one of the beast-folk.

"'Ere!" said that one, losing his pseudo-cultured accents. "Wot's the idear, sloshing a chap about!"

"Stow it," said the Colonel. "We can see you, you know. No use keeping up a pretense, old troll!"

Good for the Colonel!

"That's right," said I. "For the record, you're a lumpy-looking piece of dough, greenish-orange, with a tinge of maroon at the moment because you're mad. Madder'n usual, I mean. You blighters live in a constant state of ire, don't you?" Then I bellowed. "Stop him!" for the brute was edging toward the window. Alec picked up a small chair and tossed it at his legs, and as he tripped and went to his knees, John tapped him lightly but sternly on the head with a big glass ashtray. The alien sat cross-legged on the floor and glared wickedly at us, its true body quaking and shivering with wrath, "Well?" it said, through its robot's mouth. "Well?"

"First off," said I, strolling over to it and keeping a careless attitude tight-drawn about a wildly beating heart, "you'll answer us a few questions. Then...we'll see."

"I *don't* think," said the other.

It was brutal, but entirely excusable. I picked him off the floor—he was a slight, insignificant fellow—and hit him squarely on the nose. He catapulted backwards with a howl. Alec thoughtfully kicked him in the stomach.

"The idea, you see," I told him, "is to hurt you badly, but to keep you alive. For a while, anyway. And if you try that again," I roared, for the beast had given a kind of preliminary shrug of its real form in preparation for leaving this dimension, "if you make one more move like that, I'll murder you instanter—and you'll die, both you and that poor shell of yours. Won't you?"

It nodded sullenly. Its great amorphous being settled down into itself quietly, as the human massaged his stomach.

"Whereas," I went on, "if you're good, and answer a few queries, *maybe* I'll let you go back into the silver land of your own free will, before I slay that husk you've appropriated."

IT watched me for a while, speculating. Then it said hoarsely, "Which of you is Robert Hood of Manchester? You?" pointing at me.

"That's right, chum."

"How did you find him?" asked Geoff. "How'd you follow him?"

The brute turned its marionette's head toward our blind companion, sneered, and said nothing. I would not have this draff, this otherworld swine, sneering at Geoff; I lashed out and knocked him galley-west. Sniveling, he crawled up onto a straight-backed chair and sat there, peering round at us until his eyes lit on Marion.

"'Ere, miss," he whined. "You won't see 'em beat a poor chap to death, will you? I've done you no harm..."

I was proud of my girl then. I had been afraid our battering of the beast would set her teeth on edge; but she leaned forward and spat invective into its face. "You foul, filthy spawn of a Gadarene hog! I'd see you sliced to fringes, and laugh for joy!"

It sank back and regarded the carpet bleakly.

"How'd you follow the Slasher?" asked Geoff again.

"We all had his description. It was known he was in or near London. Then he was seen in a restaurant nearby. Our comrade lost him in Baker Street. We've been searching ever since." The voice was now too expressionless even to be called cold. "The others will find you. It doesn't matter what you do to me."

"Aha," I snapped, "except to *you!* We can feel your fear, you know." It was true; he was loathsomely afraid. It gave me a good feeling, one of renewed confidence, to realize afresh that the usurpers were not omnipotent godlings, but beings who, like any others, could know fear. Again I thought I saw the thing pull himself up surreptitiously, like a man caught in the mire; and again I slapped his head sideways till his jaws grated. He stopped it.

"Next," said the Colonel, "what are you doing here? Your race, I mean. What d'you want with this earth? It isn't yours, dammit."

The beast looked at him. Then it laughed. Somehow it managed to get a shade of the horror of its own being into the vocal chords of the puppet, and the laugh was icy. It did not answer.

So the Colonel and Alec and I worked it over. We formed a triangle, like bullies persecuting a small boy, and threw it from one to the other, not really injuring it, but slapping its face and pummeling it until it shrieked hysterically. Then we let it sink to the floor, and we tried again.

"What are you doing here?"

I HAD been afraid that we would never find this out, or that, if one of them told us, we would not be able to understand; perhaps the concept, the point of view, would seem as wild and bizarre and incredible as *they* themselves. But as it began to speak now, I found that its motives, those of all its uncanny race, were as plain and nearly human as could be.

"We found your land by accident," it said, nursing its head in its hands and speaking without inflection or accent. "I do not know how long ago it was by your standards. I think a long time. One of our people by a mischance of a kind I cannot describe in the words of your language was born into your dimension in conjunction with an infant of your race. When you are all dead, and we are the sole owners of both our dimensions and yours, and write history books here for our amusement even as you have done for your own, that chance birth will be hailed as joyfully and reverently as you hail the—discovery of America."

"Dashed if I hail *that* reverently," murmured the Colonel. "Bloomin' colonials…go on."

"I wonder if you can imagine with what delight our people greeted the discovery? How far can you see into our plane?"

I SAW no harm in answering that.

"Not far. Just a background of silver-blue lines at an angle."

"That is it. A silver land." Evidently they had the same color perception as we; a surprising but not wholly unthinkable fact. "Nowhere is there color or change of form or beauty, save in our own bodies. Your earth burst on our ken with such a wealth of beauty and such opportunities for pleasure as we had never dreamt of. At once we began to infiltrate, in the guise of normal humans; at first only by the route of births stemming from that original accident, then afterwards by births regulated and controlled from our plane, by methods you could not comprehend, which once discovered freed us from the necessity of waiting endlessly to be born into a body that had descended from that original fortuitous 'sport.' I believe that in terms of your space-time continuum, this discovery of ours has been quite recent."

I grew pale and cold at his words.

For—if true—this meant that the beast-folk could make a wholesale invasion of our dimension at any time! The brute saw me, and laughed again.

"Exactly. You are beaten. Indeed, you never had a chance, but now you have less than none. We are an advance guard, who have prepared the way for all the others of our race who will one day inhabit bodies on your plane. We have felt you out, tested your power to resist—which has been practically nil, my friend, with the exception of your own feeble and haphazard efforts—and spread out over this island until we are more numerous than you can imagine. But with the new method of coming in, there is no longer a need for infiltrating into high offices and key government positions, as we have so laboriously done before; for, my friend, D-Day is at hand."

HE folded his arms and chuckled once more, icily, hideously. "Quite soon now, we will come into this dimension in one great wave that will obliterate your race as though the stars had never shone upon it at all! Every birth in the world shall be one of our robots—and then, no matter how you struggle and fume and plot, your people are doomed! Then, no matter how hard you fight, you will lose, for your species will ultimately die of old age!"

In the silence that followed this burst of ghoulish amusement, I heard someone who was going by in Baker Street whistling the Bronze Horse Overture, one of my favorites…oddly, irrelevantly, I considered it a good omen, and was cheered. Then Geoff spoke.

"Just put my hands on his throat, somebody, will you?"

"Not yet, son. Go on, ogre. Why will you murder a whole race? Just for amusement? Just so you can see colors and pretty forms?"

"Yes. That simple a reason. And because we hate you, for that you have inherited a world of such perfections and do not appreciate it. To see colors, to revel in sounds and scents and tastes we had never imagined; to feel the vicarious ecstasy of these robots in acts you take for granted—acts of feeding, of drinking, of viewing and touching, of sex, which we do not have in our proper forms in any fashion whatever. We envy you, and hate you. We want your world, even if we must take its tactile delights vicariously—which is not so second-best as it sounds, for these robots are in a sense ourselves as much as our own bodies are. You who are born to this wondrousness—can you claim you properly appreciate it? Or will you admit that you have held it lightly and unthinkingly for as many generations as you can count?"

"Well, I'll be a devaluated pound," gasped Alec. "Will you listen to the conceited son-of-a-bitch!"

"Another question," I said to the beast. "How do—"

It was done almost before I could blink. He made a sudden break for the windows, one arm raised to smash the glass so that he could shout down to the street. Two feet short of his goal he ran into Alec's good right hand, swung round like the head of a short-hafted axe. He dropped with a crash.

"No use inspecting the body," I said. "His real shape blew up like a paper bag and went blam. I guess you broke his neck. He's dead."

Geoff stood up and said matter-of-factly, "Well, we'd best be going, what? If someone will just find my pipe for me, I'm ready."

"Wait till I toss a few things into my purse," said Marion, "Can't expect a gal to flee without a lipstick, can you?"

I stared at Alec; who nodded. It was time for us to be on the wing.

CHAPTER SEVENTEEN

AFTER three or four minutes of stuffing useful things into our pockets and a couple of overnight bags, we went downstairs to the ground floor; turning toward the back door, we ran smack into a sentinel of the usurpers. He wavered, then stepped aside as we strode toward him. I did not want to make a scene in The Gander, so waited until we stood in the lane behind the inn before I told them we had been seen.

"Never thought we wouldn't be," said the Colonel. "Where's the garage, Alec?"

It was directly opposite the rear of the inn. We went in and, unmolested, packed ourselves into the great red Rolls. "Whither?" said I, taking over the wheel.

"The Albany. I've guns there we'll need before we're much older."

"Then to the Gloucester," said Alec, "for Johnson."

I swung out into the lane and nearly ran down an alien, who leaped squeaking out of the way. Now they knew what our car looked like. I didn't care. We seemed to be in over our heads already.

"Do you know that in an hour or two we'll be much-wanted fugitives from the horrid vengeance of Scotland Yard?" I asked as we reared downtown. "We left a corpse on the floor of Alec's sitting room, with enough of our gear lying around to identify us all. My God! We're acting like a pack of heedless cretins. We should have stayed and made a plan."

"Hark to the Manchester Slasher!" shouted Geoff. "Why, my dear old cloth-head, the late lamented's buddies would have been on us in force in less than two ticks. Have you forgotten that somewhere in their dimension, at a spot approximating the location of Alec's flat, there's a dead beast-critter? Their pony express would ha' found him first thing. We had to run. And I didn't hear you objectin', when we snatched up Marion's intimate garments and Alec's dirty socks, to doing a bunk."

"My mind seems to be running ten minutes behind time," I said, skirting a corner and just missing a little old lady.

"Also there's this," put in the doctor. "We could never have gotten rid of the body, but *they* could, and I believe they will. They know now there's at least half a dozen of us in this business. Do you think they'll want us brought to trial? Granted that our story would sound like half a ton of wet fish...would they want it spread on the front pages? After all, they can tell by our looks we're solid citizens. We *might* get some credence from the police—the last thing *they* would want. I think they'll quietly haul away that body, and set out on our trail by themselves. The time for worrying about the law is over, as I see it. There's too many of us. It wouldn't be like hauling up just one ripper with a mad story; it would mean publicity in every paper in Christendom—will *they* risk that?"

"Good for you, john," I said. "You're right. It's them and us now."

WE drew up at the Albany. Leaving Geoff and Marion in the car, the four of us hurried to the Colonel's rooms and began a systematic collection of weapons, even including a set of ancient Khattar daggers and a couple of pig-sticking spears which were part of a collection Bedford had made in India. Into a Gladstone we stuffed bottles of brandy and whisky, a first aid kit, such items of clothing as we'd need in our flight, and what looked like seven years' supply of ammunition. Down again and through the lobby we went, trying to look like eccentrics who habitually carried sporting rifles, elephant guns and pig-sticking lances under our arms when we ambled through the city; piled the stuff onto the floor of the tonneau, wedged in once more, ran down to the Gloucester to get Sergeant Johnson, and took the road out of London to the east. As the sun was setting we left the last suburb behind, and came to the quiet open countryside.

"Where now?" I asked.

"The castle?" suggested Geoff. "It's as good a hideout as any."

So, after a vote, we struck out for Exeter Castle.

CHAPTER EIGHTEEN

IT was dark when we passed through Exeter Parva. So far as we could tell, there had been no pursuit; nevertheless I felt nervous and on edge, remembering what titanic forces were arrayed against us.

The elms and oaks and chestnuts whispered among themselves as we unloaded our gear and hauled it through the great iron-banded door to stack it in the empty hall. I was standing in the doorway looking at the dark groves and the moors beyond, when Marion touched my arm.

"Don't jump like that, boy! I only wanted to ask what you're gazing at so fiercely."

"The trees. They're like so many ghosts…darling, I feel as though we'd walked into the dim and haunted past. This might be Glamis Castle itself."

She seized my hand and for the first time in the whole adventure I knew she was afraid. "I think it's a trap," she said. "Oh, Will, I can't say anything to the others—after all, there's nowhere else to go—but I don't like this place!"

"It's not what you'd call cheerful."

"It's a great box propped up with bait under it, and now that we've walked under it, it's going to drop over us. Don't listen. I'm only scared. That awful man, this afternoon, telling us their damnable plan in that cool way—I feel like Peter Rabbit, nibbling on a cabbage leaf while the farmer cocks his shotgun."

"Pass me one of those cabbage leaves, Pete," I said, "I'm hungry!" That set her giggling, and broke the evil spell.

Lugging our weapons and bags, we followed the Colonel up the big curved staircase and down the dank passage to our old quarters. We lit a lamp or two; the familiar furniture sprang out of darkness, and my gaze fell first on the table to which the Tower musket had once been clamped. That seemed half a century ago, I dropped my pig-stickers and rifles on the table. "Let's hustle up some food."

"It's stacked in the next room," said the Colonel, who had been in charge of our stores during the first residence here. "There's enough for about three weeks."

"I'll get dinner," said Marion.

"I'll go down to the wine bins and bring up a few bottles," said Johnson. Luckily, Geoff's ancestors had laid down a noble cellar full of the finest potables.

183

WE all began bustling around, Alec dusting, Marion clinking dishes in our makeshift kitchen, the doctor arranging chairs about the table, the Colonel and I stacking weapons against the walls, and Geoff lounging in an armchair whistling a militant tune. We grew quite gay, laughing and chattering, until old Johnson came in with his pale face grown chalky. The Colonel saw him first.

"For God's sake, man, what is it?"

Johnson sat down heavily, by which sign I knew he was terribly upset, for he would never sit when the rest of us were standing. He passed a hand over his eyes. "I was going through the hall—downstairs, that is—and suddenly I felt as though someone were observing me, you know the sensation, sir?"

"Yes, yes."

"Well, I looked about, and saw nothing at first, so thinking it was my nerves, I went on to the cellars. I chose two bottles of wine and a good brandy—" he held them out and automatically I took them—"and came up again. Just as I stepped through the entrance to the cellars, I happened to glance toward the front door. There, looking in at me through the dirty glass of the window beside it was a face. I—I can't tell you what a turn it gave me. The eyes seemed almost to glow, you know, sir. It was horrible."

Into the silence that followed Geoff said, "We've had a ghost here for ten generations, Johnson. The Stalking Man, they call him. I used to see him frequently when I was a nipper. He's supposed to walk on the south terrace between sundown and cockcrow."

Johnson stared wildly at him as though Geoff had sprouted two heads. "No, no sir," he said. "This wasn't a man. It was a woman."

"What happened next?" barked the Colonel.

"Well, sir, I'm afraid I was so startled that I stepped back into the entrance-way; and when I had conquered my aversion and returned, she was gone. I didn't go and look out the window as I should. I fear I was badly rattled. I came straight upstairs."

You might have sliced the apprehension in that room with a blunt knife. Nobody moved, except to turn their heads to one another with widened eyes. I wet my lips then.

"The barmaid from Exeter Parva," I said. "They've identified Geoff from something he left behind, and sent the word down here to check on the castle. It would occur to them at once, when they knew about Geoff, that we might make for such a sanctuary. They've sent the word to that fearful green-horned octopus, and it's hared out here to investigate. We're pinpointed now, lads, like a covey of quail on an open marsh."

Colonel Bedford was holding a Mannlicher. He opened the bolt with a snap. "Load up, my boys," he said. "Load 'em all up, and then let's have some food. The condemned may as well eat a hearty meal."

CHAPTER NINETEEN

SURPRISINGLY, we all slept very well that night. Each of us (save Geoff and Marion) took an hour and a half at sentry-go, roaming through the monstrous old place peering out of windows and jumping at every creak; but before and after my own tour of duty I slept dreamlessly and comfortably, and found in the morning that the others had done likewise. We foregathered at the breakfast table, which was placed in the center of a broad cheerful beam of sunlight that lanced down through age-old panes of glass, and we ate tinned meat and biscuits with honey and mugs of well-creamed coffee, with as excellent appetites as one could wish for.

When the meal was done, Johnson picked up one of the long pig-sticking spears and hefted it, trying the balance.

"Going to stab us a shoat, Sergeant?" asked Alec.

"No, sir. It's that I can't abide firearms, while fifty years ago I was rather good with one of these, if I may say so without boasting. A number of us used to go out on the veld and try our luck at riding down small antelope. On days when the Boers left us alone, you know, sir, I think I could still wield one with the best of you young 'uns—begging your pardon, I'm sure, sir."

The Colonel bounced out of his chair. "Line up for weapons issue," he cried. "Who's tough enough to handle my elephant gun?"

"Will Chester," said Marion, with a grim nod.

I was then presented with the heaviest piece of Bedford's artillery and two pocketfuls of shells. Doctor John drew the Mannlicher and the Colonel himself took a murderous old 450-400 with which he'd once hunted big game. Marion had a light sporting rifle. Geoff and Alec, who styled themselves the Hamstrung Brigade, could obviously not handle rifles; but Alec thrust two Colt .45's through his belt, and Geoff was allowed to wear a long hunting knife "just in case." The Colonel outfitted each of us others with one or two revolvers apiece, and we parceled out plenty of ammunition. Even Johnson had to add a .22 target pistol to his brace of spears.

"Now then," said Colonel Bedford, "here's how I see it. We're in as good a place as any for hanging on: the place is unburnable, and we can hold it against successive waves—first fighting on the ground floor, then retreating to this one, hall by hall and room by room, and finally when things really grow hot we can get onto the roof and make a fight there. We're far enough away from any settlement that the noise of a battle won't carry except by a freak of the wind. We can have a nice private war."

"But," interrupted Marion, "do we want a nice private war? I think we should want publicity for it, because *they* don't. D'you see? I'm for dragging the whole mess into the open."

"And end in a loony bin," said Alec. "No, the Colonel's right as far as he goes: this is the place to make a stand, and since we know we can't escape to anywhere in this island that'll be safe, we may as well stop here to make our fight. They aren't going to bring down a blooming brigade to eliminate us, mind you; they'll think, 'Ha, there's only seven, we'll just send round a score or so to pip 'em.' They don't know we've an arsenal here."

"And meanwhile," said Geoff excitedly, waving his pipe, "Arold Smiff in Birmingham will be gathering *his* crew. If we give him—how long would you say, Will?"

"Another couple of days, maybe. He's got to treat each of those thugs to a drink or two and sound him out before he hires him. It will take a few days. Besides, he thinks he's got a week at least. I'm supposed to be meandering over England getting names. And I'm afraid that scheme's out, too."

"P'raps, p'raps…well, say we give Arold a couple of days, and then phone him—from Exeter Parva, let's say—to bring his outlaws down here a-whoopin' and a-cussin' in a bunch. How's that? They roar in, mop up practically all the usurpers in sight, then we catch a few of the aliens and tell 'em, 'This is a sample. We can see you, so there's no use your sticking. Scram!' How's that?"

"Dandy, dandy. Except for the little matter of getting out of here to phone Arold. What if we're surrounded?"

"Oh, hell's tinkling bells! Where's your red Injun blood? But if you like, one of us can leave now, before they arrive.

He can contact Arold, have him hurry it up, and in a day or two catch the besiegers in the rear." Geoff was jubilant, and some of his fervor rubbed off on me. I said, "Right! We'll draw straws."

"You're the logical choice, Will," said Alec. "You know this Smith, after all. The plan is your pigeon. You go."

The Colonel was standing by the window, glancing out now and again as we talked. He said, "One minute chaps. Come here."

We crowded to the window. He pointed down to the drive. Shortly we saw a man run stooping across an open space in the old stone balustrade. The substance of the alien body seemed to float about him like a flimsy cloak of many colors.

"They're all along the front," said Bedford. "If they've covered the back, lads—it's a bit late for our emissary to think of leaving."

We spread out over the house, peering cautiously out of windows at front and back and sides. Then we gathered in the upper hall, as disconsolate a band of crusaders as ever eyed each other with grim scowls.

We were entirely surrounded. The siege was on.

CHAPTER TWENTY

MARION and the doctor roamed the upper floor, watching developments from the windows; when the first rush came, they were to fire down on the enemies' heads. Geoff was ensconced behind an overturned table at the head of the great staircase, so he could at least hear everything that occurred. Alec, Johnson, the Colonel and I were the ground floor garrison; we bolted off the east and west wings entirely, barricading the doors thereto with piles of lumber from the cellars so that if the aliens broke into those sections of the castle, it would avail them little. We had already carried a dozen armloads of bottles up to our quarters from the bins below us, and there seemed little we could do now but wait, there in that echoing empty hall, until our foe took the initiative. This happened about eleven o'clock that morning.

We heard Marion's warning cry, and instantly sprang to our feet (we had each been sitting below a window, trying to relax) and looked out. I was at the front of the house with Alec. I saw some fifteen or eighteen of the monstrous beast-folk come lumbering across the open spaces between the house and the drive. I smashed a pane of glass in the mullioned window with my elephant gun and let fly at the foremost surper. He caught the charge right in the belly, and went heels-over-head backward to lie in a tangle of dark limbs and body, above which the mortally wounded alien grew pale and flickered and went out with a sputter. I let off the second barrel at another and reloaded hastily, thanking the powers that I'd taken this great shoulder-punishing gun rather than one of the lighter and less effective rifles; its load would stop a man even if the wound was not mortal, and I with my double vision was handicapped above my friends. It was often difficult for me to locate the vital points in a running puppet, when the body about him was distending and wavering through half-a-dozen horrible shapes.

I stopped another pair of them in as many seconds, then drew my two revolvers and began to fire first one and then the other, ambidextrously, like Wild Bill Hickock in the films. I don't know how many shots I wasted, but it was a bloody barrage.

THAT first charge lasted no more than three minutes, I should judge. They were taken quite by surprise, and comparing notes after, we discovered that they had not even bothered to have their own guns drawn when they began their attack. They must have pictured us crouching in terror, with bottles and chair legs for weapons.

Marion came to the head of the stairs and called to us. We assured her of our safety; Geoff was growling to himself over not being able to take a hand in the sport. Then the second wave came at us.

This time they were more cautious, and had automatics and target pistols in their hands. We took toll of them with our rifles and then with our handguns; when they withdrew again, they left at least a score of dead and dying husks on the ground around our fortress.

Just to show them that we were the seers they thought us, and also to decimate the ranks of the ungodly, I picked off all those wounded robots whose tenants were vacating, dashing back and forth from window to window to give the effect of half a dozen sharpshooters. I think that gave them pause, for nothing else happened until well into the afternoon.

Alec had a grazed cheek from which the blood was seeping, and Johnson had been cut on the shoulder by flying glass, but otherwise we were still intact.

"What do they look like?" I asked Alec, as we stood together watching the deserted drive. "I can't tell much from those crumpled corpses, and you know they're so many dim shadows in misshapen sheaths of unearthly coloring to me when they're alive."

"Oh, they're—normal. People you'd see anywhere, and never notice 'em. Small business men, maybe, or out-of-work clerks. Nondescript. Certainly they're not seasoned fighters."

"It's occurred to me that a lot of *them* must have got out of joining in the late world fracas, one way or another; through their bigwigs, you know. I doubt they'd care to go marching off to war in one of our little two-bit three-dimensional fracases, and I'll bet their ranks were full of shirkers and slackers and dodgers and pseudo-conchies. So maybe they have no experienced fighters!"

"Those out there aren't," agreed Alec. "What duffers they looked, trotting up to our guns!"

THERE was one more attack, about four o'clock. This was a more carefully planned affair, and by utilizing all the cover they could, and coming in from all directions, they managed to get right up to the windows. When they did we retreated to the center of the hall; the windows framed them into perfect targets, and after losing a dozen or more they retreated in their turn, for the last time that day.

At dusk we deserted the ground floor and, barricading the stairs as effectively as we could, took up our posts on the upper floor. Sentry duty was apportioned, and after a good meal and an hour of desultory talking we lay down to sleep as much of the night through as the usurpers would allow.

My watch was from three to four-thirty. I was prowling around the halls, peering into each room as I passed, when above the night noises and the snoring of the Colonel I thought I heard an ominous creaking. On tiptoe I went down the hall, past the stairwell that went down into sinister blackness, and fetched up some yards thereafter before a gaping square hole in the wall of the passageway. What the devil...! I turned the beam of my electric torch into it. It was another staircase, narrow and steep, which I had not known existed. Without hesitation I started down its creaky old treads. The air was musty and smelled of a thousand generations of mice. More through my skin than my ears I got the impression that someone was descending these secret stairs in advance of me.

I drew out one of my guns, with a childlike thrilling of my pulse, and muffling the torch's light with the fingers of my left hand so that only a thin streak or two of brightness preceded my searching feet, I went down.

The square door at the bottom was standing wide. Slipping through it, with the torch now dark, I stood still and listened.

THE moon's rays patterned the cold floor under the windows, and across one of them I thought I saw a shadow glide. I swiveled my head quickly. Perhaps I had been mistaken. There was nothing there. The end of the room in which was cradled the massive black fireplace lay in impenetrable gloom. Watching this, I felt the skin of my neck creep and the hair bristle...

Something had moved in that murk, I could swear it. Something bigger and more ponderous than a body. I could not pin down the exact analogy I groped for: it was as if...as if the wall had suddenly advanced toward me, and then sunk back again. I husked through a dry throat. This would not do. Despite the usurpers without, I had to risk a light.

I shot the beam of the torch across the wall from corner to corner. Nothing moved. I went to the cold fireplace— feeling the eyes of a multitude of ghosts upon me as I moved—and ran the flash over it. I even knelt and peered up the gut of the chimney. Nothing. I found myself shuddering. One more sweep of the torch around the vault of the hall, and then I ran (I admit it freely) for the secret door. Pulling it to behind me, I raced up the narrow steps and with pounding heart slammed the upper one also. I saw then that it was a swinging panel that looked much like anyone of the other panels in the hall. This secret must be a relic of the bad old days, when Exeter Castle was young and the nobility was riddled with treachery, intrigue, and evil.

After two minutes of cogitation, I went and aroused Colonel Bedford. He listened to my tale in silence. Then, "This might be serious," he said. "Let's wake the others."

We did, and in the short time before the early dawn of summer gilded the east windows, we combed that castle from roof to cellars; but the incredible fact, which we had uncovered, remained, not to be dispelled or explained by any means in our power.

Geoff Exeter, our poor gallant blind Geoff, had disappeared...

CHAPTER TWENTY-ONE

I truly believe that that day was the longest and worst I ever managed to live through.

The aliens who ringed the castle did not attack in force; but they maintained a kind of sullen, dangerous watchfulness over the place, and every time one of us showed himself at a window, a rifle cracked and a slug spread itself on a wall nearby or buried itself in the ceiling above him.

"What are they doing?" Marion asked me again and again. "Why are they waiting?" And I could not tell her.

The night came, but our sleep was no more than an occasional leaden doze, which left us unrefreshed, with gummy aching eyes and minds gnawed by worry.

Where in hell was Geoff?

Had they slipped in and abducted him, right out from beneath our noses? Hardly. The doors and windows were still bolted.

Had he left of his own free will? And if so, *how*? And why?

"The place is haunted," Alec had said somberly at dinner; and in my heart I half agreed with him.

That night we had renewed our barricades at the head of the stairs, and kept our watches as before. About six in the morning I was starting to tear down the lumber once more when a hand was laid on my arm, and the Colonel, his face gray and drawn, said, "Leave 'em, boy."

"Why?"

"Come and look out the window. They've gathered. There must be two hundred if there's a one. We can't hold that great hall against them when they come. We've got to make a stand up here."

It was true. The groves and the unkempt lawns swarmed with them, their loathsome bodies all gay and shining in the sunlight.

"Still clerks and shopkeepers?" I asked.

"No, this is a rather less appetizing lot. More like the mugs you were always spying on in pubs," said Alec. "They look—well, pretty competent."

"We'll give them a reception," said the Colonel grimly. "Spread out, front and back, and fire into the brown of 'em when I give the word. Empty your rifles and then your revolvers as fast as you can; the fools are bunched so that we can't miss. There's not a military man in the lot. I'll be bound."

I went to the farthest corner of the east wing, many rooms away from our G. H. Q. by the main stairwell; I swung open a window as gently as possible, then waited for the Colonel's signal. I imagined he would fire his 450-400. I was forgetting that for development of the lungs there's nothing to compare with half a lifetime of commanding the sepoys of India. To say merely that he shouted "Fire!" in a stentorian voice is like saying that the Last Trump will be rather loud. His bellow rattled the beams of oak in their stone sockets. Even the aliens on the lawns turned to look in his direction.

I thrust out the muzzle of my pachyderm blaster and let it speak twice in rapid fire; dropped it, threw down on the milling crew with my two Colts, and picked off three more usurpers before they could gather their wits and make for the groves. When the guns were empty I counted seven bodies. If my friends had had as good luck, I thought exultantly, the foe had lost more than thirty of their number! I found subsequently that our total for the surprise attack was twenty-four or-five.

This decimation must have shaken them to their toes, for the morning wore on and no assault came.

Johnson brought each of us a bowl of soup and a plate of biscuits at noon. Staying at my post in the eastern corner. I watched the trees and thought of Geoff Exeter.

Could that have been Geoff whom I followed down the secret stair two nights since? Certainly it was not one of *them*; and Geoff of all people would have known of its existence, for he had spent his childhood here in the castle. If it was him, where had he gone from the great hall? And what had moved in the black shadows of the fireplace? Had Geoff been spirited away by ghosts? I could credit anything, after these past months of hellish experience.

As I was chewing my last biscuit, firing broke out at the front of the castle; first a single shot or two, then heavy volleys, as though all my friends were engaged in it. I shifted from foot to foot, wondering what to do. Finally, after a searching look at the groves and lawns where nothing moved, I ran for the hallway.

MARION and Alec were shooting from the windows of our sitting room. I dashed in, said foolishly, "What is it, an attack?" and looking out saw line after line of the beast-folk advancing rapidly on the castle, their numbers not bunched this time but spread out so that they presented more difficult targets. I judged them to be at least two hundred and fifty strong. "Shoot low," I snapped, even as I brought the elephant gun to bear on a blue octopus-like brute and sent him sprawling. "Remember you're aiming downhill."

The thunder of a battering ram smiting at the big door seemed to jar the floor beneath our feet. It ceased in a moment, and I heard the Colonel bawl, "They're in! Come to the stairs!"

We gathered there behind our lumber-and-furniture barricade, six against an army. We did not say anything coherent, I believe, but continually shouting encouraging noises to one another, we fired and fired until our weapons grew hot to the touch. The beasts were thronging the hall below us, converging on the stairs and tearing at the mass of impeding obstacles which the Colonel and John had strewn down the length of the steps that morning. It was at once a hideous and a thrilling sight. The monsters were swarming up at us, a foot at a time, clawing at planks and barrels and broken chairs, hurling them back onto their comrades' heads; none of them seemed to be firing at us, though in the heat of battle I may not have noticed if they had. It looked to me as if they were too infuriated to bother with guns. Like so many enraged baboons, they wanted to get at us and tear us to bloody tatters with their hands and teeth alone. As they fought upward, those in the fore exploded soundlessly, horribly, and quickly, like multicolored bags of gaudy rubber stabbed with sharp knives, leaving their dead robots to roll and flounder to the bottom again. I had run out of ammo for the big gun; howling with a kind of mad glee, I blazed away into the thick of them with my twin Colts, putting my bullets into the dark human forms within the hybrid monsters. The castle rocked and echoed with the fury of the fight. Cordite and spilt blood reeked in my nostrils. One of the devils, a rhinocerous-brute with a towering ivory-tinted "horn" that wobbled as he moved, came scrambling on all fours up over the mess of wreckage toward us; I took him for my very own, waiting until he was within a yard of me and then presenting both my revolvers to his face, pulled the triggers.

My guns were empty!

BEFORE I could recover from my surprise, he had gathered himself—he must have been an especially athletic fellow—and leaped straight for me. I went down under his weight, flailing my arms wildly. I was unprepared for a scuffle and for a few seconds could do nothing to defend myself properly. Before I had rallied, the body of the creature went limp and sagged down onto me, while his true form flickered away into nothingness. I struggled out from under him to see old Johnson pulling back a bloodied pig-sticker. He grinned at me complacently. "Still a trace of the old skill left, Mister Chester!"

They were the last words he ever spoke. A volley crashed out below us, and he swayed and fell at full length, like an ancient tree cut at the roots. I knelt over him, and saw that he was dead.

I peered over the railing, while feverishly loading my guns, and saw that we were nearly done; for the aliens, sacrificing scores of their men in that wild attack, had almost cleared the staircase. Now they were pulling back the corpses and the last of the impeding furniture, and only our barricade at the top remained between them and our garrison of five. Any of them who were in good shape and in the least degree agile could clear this barrier with ease, I knew we were almost done.

Now there occurred one of those queer, inexplicable pauses that come in the thick of the wildest battles, when the men of both sides seem to draw back an imperceptible inch or two, cease firing and yelling, suck in a deep swift breath, and tauten their muscles for a final foray or a last furious defense. The usurpers in the hall and on the stairs fell silent as though by prearrangement; while we humans, as it chanced, were all either loading or taking careful sights over our gun barrels.

And in that comparative silence, broken only by the susurrus of heavy breathing, we all suddenly pricked up our ears and listened. The pause lengthened, by a sort of unspoken mutual agreement between the two parties. I looked at the Colonel, and he gestured imperiously toward the nearest room that faced on the drive. I flew into it, making for a window.

Because there had come to us the sound of many automobiles, driven at high speed down the country lane that led to Exeter Castle.

CHAPTER TWENTY-TWO

BEHIND me I heard firing start up again, though not with any great volume. Below me as I leaned out of the window I saw a number of usurpers come running out of the broken door to see what was happening, then turn and go in again. My attention was not on them however, but on the drive, where the first of a line of motors had already pulled up and stopped.

It was an old pre-war sedan. Its doors opened and six or seven men boiled out of it, staring at the castle and shouting as they moved.

Men! Not were-folk, not monsters, but *men!*

Had the sound of our fight carried to Exeter Parva? No, it could never produce these fifteen autos, decrepit though most of them were. Exeter Parva ran more to hay wagons.

Then the riddle was solved. The second car, a battered Bentley, halted, and out of the front seat climbed a man I would have recognized on a dark night in a cellar.

Dear old drunken, amoral, faithful Arold Smiff! Smiff to the rescue!

"At 'em, Arold!" I whooped. "Inside, son!"

He stared up at me, then waved joyfully. "General! Hoy, General! Gawddam!" He motioned fiercely to his henchmen. "Come on, you one-legged paralyzed barstids, earn your wack! Out arms and forrard!"

Great God, did ever such a motley army advance on such an unearthly enemy? It was like the thieves of Paris defending their city against Burgundy...had that kingdom recruited its army from the swamps of Hell. From the line of cars swarmed a gang of shabby, dirty, swearing men, as tough and evil looking a mob as ever trod the soil of England. Spawned in the slums and reared on violence, every one of them! Muggers, knifers, coshers, men with scarred faces and broken teeth, men fitting brass knuckles on their fists as they came, men sliding straight razors (the favorite weapon of our underworld) from their frayed sleeves and clicking open big clasp knives, men drawing automatics for which you could have staked your life they had no permits, men who were scarcely more than wild boys and men who had grown gray and bald in crime; at once as undisciplinable and as effective a fighting troop as one could find anywhere. I think I screamed encouragement to them as they came, for I was half-hysterical with relief. Arold Smiff, miraculously, had come in time.

AS they ran toward the castle I ducked inside and went to my friends, loading my guns as I moved. The aliens were still attacking up the stairs, but now they wavered as the vanguard of the thugs struck them from behind. All roaring hell broke loose.

I saw plenty of action in the last war; I saw the slaughter of the Normandy beaches and the havoc wrought through France, Germany, and several other countries; but the goriest brawl I ever laid eye on was the fight at Exeter Castle between Arold Smiff's hundred criminals and the motley hordes of the silver land.

We were outnumbered, at the start, nearly two to one. But our crooks were professional killers, used to the mechanics of murder, and the usurpers were not. The hall was jammed from wall to wall with a struggling, howling, thrashing jam of fighters, so that often when a man was killed his body could not fall; conditions were thus perfect for our knifers and gougers, throttling experts and razormen.

The aliens for the most part had turned from us to engage this new menace. We tore away our barricade and charged down to mix it with them. I caught a glimpse of Arold before I struck the level. He had an automatic in his right hand and in his left, one of those fearsome weapons used by the gangs in their private wars, called a "moley"—a large potato, stuck half-full of safety razor blades. When pressed against the face and twisted, it made a grisly instrument of torture, mutilation, and often death. I grimaced. These were wicked men who had come to our rescue.

With our heavy Colts we blasted back the beast-men till we had cleared a space at the foot of the stairs; standing shoulder to shoulder, we bellowed, "Rally! To us, to us, rally round!" and many of the rogues fought through the press to join us, so that shortly we were the nucleus of the battle. Bedford led a charge that smashed the center of the enemy line and crumpled up the right wing as it returned. I saw John Baringer go down from a blow on the head; beat my way to him and dragged him to the relative safety of the big fireplace.

I was entirely out of ammunition by then. Sticking the pistols in my belt for last-ditch use as clubs, I grappled with the human husk of a big sprawling beetle-beast, throttled him, took away a butcher's cleaver he was utilizing, brained him with it and waded into the combat once more. I was splashed with gore from boots to hair, my left arm was numb from a crack on the elbow, I was whooping like a maniac, and felt myself supremely happy. I would not have been anywhere else for ten thousand pounds sterling.

I found myself next to Arold. I hugged him, and his muddy-crimson eyes squeezed up with a grin. "General! Bloody fine scrim!"

"How did you know to come here?" I yelled at him; but the tides of battle flung us apart before he could answer. I knew, though. Nobody in the world but Geoff could have brought him.

I found myself engaged with a razorman of our own forces, and had to explain who I was, in exceedingly rapid speech. Then I went hunting for the Colonel, and found him dripping blood (someone else's) by the stairs. Now the fight had become a massacre, and the aliens, fleeing, found a heavy guard on the door and no sanctuary anywhere short of the grave. "Colonel," I screeched in his ear, "your voice will carryover this hubbub. Go up the stairs a bit—tell 'em to leave a few alive—got to parley!"

He clumped up the steps, and his bull's roar quelled the racket like thunder drowning out a kindergarten choir. The thugs turned astonished eyes upward, and the few usurpers still on their feet shrank together in a corner. For one brief instant I felt pity for them. Then I remembered their plot to take over our world...

"That's enough," the Colonel was saying. "Collect the remaining enemies and bring 'em here, lads."

The "lads" did so. Alec and I went up the dozen steps to join the Colonel, Marion ran down from the upper floor, and Arold Smiff pushed through his followers to wring my hand heartily. Then we all looked at the things from the silver land, and I began to speak.

CHAPTER TWENTY-THREE

THERE were sixteen of them left—sixteen out of two hundred and fifty. No wonder the castle's great hall was swimming with blood! No wonder we all looked like red Indians! "Who's the senior ghoul among you?" I asked, and a white-haired robot encased by a yellow lumpy godhelpus moved forward a little. The Colonel hissed in my ear.

"Good gad, I know that man! That's Sir Lawrence Hockling!"

"He's also a monstrous, warty, holey creature, like a lump of wormy cheese... Good afternoon, Sir Lawrence," I said loudly. "I believe you've been looking for me. I'm Robert Hood of Manchester."

"Ah yes, the Slasher." The bugaboo that was Sir Lawrence nodded briefly. "It seems we have failed to annihilate you. No matter; others will."

"No, Sir Lawrence, you fail to grasp the situation. You're finished, you invaders. You've had your fun, but now you've got to pick up and go home, and never come back. Because we can see you."

He held up his hand. "Wait, sir. We accept you as a seer, of course. There have been others—" *Jack the Ripper*, said I to myself with a chuckle—"others who have accidentally been enabled to pierce the veil between the lands. We have dealt with them, as we shall eventually with you. But your companions—let them describe us!"

The Colonel pounced on this challenge like a tiger on a goat. I was breathless, thankful that I had described at least Sir Lawrence to him. "You're a cross between a speckled cheese and a diseased bit of garbage. Lumps and bumps all over your slimy carcass!"

"Good enough," said the monster, quaking with wrath. "That will do, Colonel Bedford. I meant to say, let some of these—ah, rather unwashed gentry tell us of our true bodies."

I was turning sick with fear, the fear, that now we were done for, that now the colossal bluff would collapse. I had forgotten Arold—Arold, who could see them plain as day.

"The bloke on yer right," he shrilled, "is lyke a shark, all silvery and slick, wiff a big glow in 'is guts lyke a blurry fire. Next t' him is—welp, it's 'ard to tell, but I'd say he were a ostopus, you know, one o' them big leather things under the ocean."

"Shall I have each of them describe you all?" I leaped into the breech with a shouted challenge. "Shall we waste a couple of hours talking of your stalks and pseudopods? Or are you satisfied? Man, man, why do you think they came here, if not to crush you and your kind? Why did you fight you with such fury, if not because they can see you in all your horror?" Needless to say, Arold's ruffians were staring bug-eyed at all this incomprehensible arguing.

"Well," said Sir Lawrence, "you obviously couldn't make so many men believe in us if they couldn't see us. I simply had to make sure." Fortunately he and the others never turned round to observe the wonder on the thugs' faces. "I accept you as seers. How did you manage it? How did you warp their vision?"

"You know as well as I." *Now, Will Chester, bluff, bluff!*

"Yes," he said, "ever since we entered your world, centuries ago, we've been afraid that one day the secret of vision-tuning might be stumbled upon by some clever member of your species. The trick of it is, after all, ridiculously simple."

I snapped my fingers to show how simple it was, as I thought grimly of that antique Tower musket blasting across my eyes. But through my brain the ideas were tumbling. There *was* an easy way to change one's sight, to peer into the silver land. That made my bluff much more feasible!

"Yet it has been found too late, sirrah. We are ready to invade your plane by the millions, through every new birth that takes place on your globe. Can you, a handful of seers, wipe out so many? I think not!"

"You fool," I said coldly, "do you think I risked our whole band in this slaughter? There are men all over England now, performing that simple operation on others. There are hundreds, yes, thousands of us already. We're wise to you my boy; we've got an underground as efficient as your own. Already we're spreading to other countries. In a short time the entire world will be on guard against you—and men will be assassinating you in the dark." I let out my chest and roared it at him. I was suddenly an inspired Henry V before Agincourt, an impassioned Emile Zola addressing the jury of Dreyfus, a thundering Caesar in the Senate. Marion said later that my eyes flashed lambent flame and she thought the roof of my mouth would split. I had a great sense of my own power; I felt my frame filling with the elation of a true savior, a liberator, an emancipator. I curved my hands like talons and shook them above my head, intoxicated with a belief in my own wholly untrue words.

"DON'T you see how useless it will be for you to be born into a world where you will be seen and immediately slain?

From now on, the bestowing of double vision will be as much a part of a man's life as his—his education, baptism, and what-have-you.   Forevermore we'll be on guard against you.   I tell you now: go home, go back to your silver-lined wastes, and never try to trouble us again.   Give up your infiltrating, your bestial usurping of bodies that ought to have had the chance to live and see and feel and think for themselves.   Go home.   God damn you all, go home!   Your sole weapon, invisibility, is gone.   You don't enjoy death any more than we do—I've felt your fear!   I feel it now!   Be sensible; you made a good try, but you've lost.   Go home!"

The mouldy-looking thing that was Sir Lawrence began to collogue silently with his countrymen, after their fashion.   I looked beyond them to the army of thugs.   Most of them, giving up their attempt to understand what the toffs were talking about, were engaged in looting the dead.   I wondered what to do with them after this was over, if my bluff worked. Pay them off and send them home, I supposed.   They would never talk about this pogrom—they'd be hanged!   I'd have to see that they helped us bury all these corpses, alien robots and dead rogues alike, before they left.   About twenty of the thugs had been killed.   Who would miss them?   And an event was coming—I devoutly hoped!—which would engulf any such minor event as the disappearance of some three hundred men from all walks of life...

At last Sir Lawrence Hockling turned back to me.   All his companions, too, faced my way.

NEVER, in all my journeying among their foul kind, had I felt the concentrated effluvia of so much hate, so many noxious, diabolic waves of damnable ferocity beating against me like the wind off the Styx, turning me weak and sick. Malignant powers from the poisonous womb of Hell!   I shook with uncontrollable nausea, with the dreadful revulsion caused by the towering, smashing, soul-wrenching blast of hatred flung at me by the group of beast-folk in that moment. It was beyond words. Nor was it my warped vision, affecting my other senses in the relatively mild way it had done before this. No, this was a feral force, a raging thing that knew no bonds of dimension or of the senses. It stabbed to the soul itself. Marion gave a muffled scream and huddled down on the step, clasping my knees; even the Colonel, the last man to be disturbed by an abstruse sensation, gasped audibly. As for poor Arold, he sat down with a bump and hid his face in his hands, whimpering; having as we did the added receptivity, that terrible blow nearly killed us both. The hall was blotted from my sight, a gulf opened below me, I felt myself hurtling down into unmentionable depths of agony. When I opened my eyes I did not know what to expect: perhaps the unknown wastes and plains of the silver land, whither their foul thrust, I thought, might very well have hurled me. As a matter of fact, I was still standing upright on the staircase. I have never been more surprised.

Then I saw that they were in the process of leaving their human bodies, wrenching and hauling backward as though caught in a tight box.

"We accept your ultimatum," said the scholarly voice of the beast who was Sir Lawrence Hockling. "We are rational beings. We have been beaten, and we will return to our own plane, which lies at an angle to your space-time continuum. Please spread the word of the capitulation abroad, so that no more may die. Agreed?"

"Agreed," I said. I leaped down the steps to stand face to face with his robot. "I give you three days of grace," I cried, "and then we begin to slay you all over England."

I looked from him to the others of that group of inferno-bred ogres, shining like so many luminous bloated corpses at the bottom of the sea, with the colors of malice and savagery changing, coming and going in their rotten bodies; feeling the last exhalations of their enmity touching me like a palpable force. It had not begun to dawn on me that we had won. My head throbbed and racketed like a gourd full of thunder. Then I saw two men coming toward me through the mob, and my headache died to a near-forgotten dull throb; for they were John Baringer and Geoff Exeter.

"Look what I found on the lawn," said the doctor. "Sitting out there as calm as ice, whistling Lili Marlene!"

"What ho," said Geoff, groping with his hand until I had gripped it with mine. "You boys have fun?"

"I knew it," said I. "I knew you were the one. How'd you get out? How'd you find your way to Birmingham?"

"Long story, son everyone okay?"

"All but Johnson."

"The sergeant," said Geoff blankly. "Why, he's to live forever, hang it."

"He's gone."

Geoff was still for a minute, and then burst out, "Well, don't say it like a morbid stuffed owl! After fifty years of civilian life, he smelt the powder and heard the shots again, God be thanked! So he died—so bloody what? It's how he *should* have gone."

"Right," said I, from the heart. I turned to the aliens then, and found sixteen grinning, drooling, mindless carcasses, staring round with blank dull eyes. They were empty hulks. The usurpers were gone into their silver-blue fastnesses, and the fight was done.

CHAPTER TWENTY-FOUR

A week had gone by. The seven of us sat over our dessert in London's finest dining room: Arold Smiff well-scrubbed and ill at ease, Geoff cheerful as ever, Alec busy savoring the coffee, John cynical again, Colonel Bedford complacent and stolid, my Marion all radiant and lovely, and myself, the erstwhile most savage one-man crime wave since Genghis Khan was a pup, fiddling with the silverware and feeling rather mournful, now that all was over.

At first we spoke of the past, as though each of us hated to think of a future apart from his companions. We asked one another questions of which we had heard the answers a dozen times before. Geoff told again how he had wandered down the secret stair that night, feeling his way along the walls, lonely and worried, and how he had remembered as he came to the ground floor that there was an old hidden exit in the back of the fireplace.

"I give you my word I never meant to use it! I only wanted to see if I remembered the trick of it. You twist one of the hounds on the stone coat of arms, and the door opens behind the logs. Well, I did it, and heard the door clink open; I hadn't tried it since I was a kid, and I thought, by golly, what a lark to go through the underground tunnel and see if the other end's still workable! I guess I had some vague notion of us using it for an escape route, if things got too hot for us in the castle. So I went in, and closed the door behind me.

"I bumbled along the tunnel—how I recalled the feel of those damp, rough bricks!—and came after three hundred feet to the other end, where a hidden trap leads to a summerhouse. I lifted it cautiously, still with no idea of leaving the tunnel, and felt the breeze on my face; and I knew then that I had to go on. I'd come this far and suddenly I knew I had to keep travelin' till I got to Birmingham and Arold. So I slipped out and cut straight through the woods till I came to the road. My lack of sight was no handicap, because there's not a chunk of turf within five miles o' the castle I don't know by its first name.

"AFTER I hit the road it was easy. I just groped my way for a few hours till I knew by the sound of the farm dogs that I'd come to Granny Moore's place. After running into a fence and a cart or two, I found the door and banged on it; explained to Granny that I had to get to Birmingham as quick as possible; and she, bless her staunch old soul, detailed her youngest boy (a lad of forty-nine) to take me there, without so much as a single query as to my reasons—and that's all. I found Arold that afternoon at Old Mag's."

"To think I was standing in the hall when you went through the door in the fireplace," I said. "God! I thought it was ghosts I heard."

"I'd have left a note, or come back to tell you, but I was all carried away with the spirit of rollicking adventure and looniness," said Geoff, filling his pipe. "I expect I gave you some bad hours. I'm sorry."

"Forgiven," gruffed the Colonel. "You saved our bacon."

"And the world," said Marion quietly.

"Yes, the world! The jolly old human race, that didn't even know it was in danger, and wouldn't believe it now if we told it! Hell's sweet bells, it's hard for *me* to believe!" Geoff laughed. "Did we really pit ourselves against ten thousand fantastic beasts, and drive them from our dimension by a colossal bluff? Or did we dream a long horrid dream, we seven strange crusaders?"

"I begin already to doubt my memory," answered Doctor John. "I was never cut out for a cavalier, wooing weird adventures. I'm a solid citizen. I'm going back to my practice on the steamers."

"When?" I asked.

"Next week." Now the present had intruded in our talk, and the future. "What will you do, Colonel?"

"Been thinking of retiring to the country, but I doubt I could stick it after all the excitement we've been through. I expect I'll stay on at the Albany. Lots of things happening about one, you know, keep a chap young."

I laughed to myself at the thought of the staid old-fashioned Albany being a beehive of activity, but said nothing. John went on. "You, Alec, what will you do?"

"Huh? Me? Dunno," said Alec blankly. "Haven't cogitated on it."

"Me neither," said Geoff.

"Marion and Will will marry, of course," said the Colonel, as though that accounted for us forever, and no question about it. "And you, sir," he said to Arold, making that worthy leap in his chair, "what do you intend doing? You're a fairly well-to-do man now."

"Ah, yes, thanks to you gents! As generous and kindly a lot o' toffs—that is to say, gentlemen—as you could arsk for. Me? I'm going over the border. Scotland, that's the ticket for Arold Smiff; nice little village, cozy house, new name, and plenty of gin—welp, anyway, I'm going to Scotland. Never meet nobody there who'd know me, and that's 'ow I wants it after the killings we done down at that there cawstle. Some of the blokes I 'ad to enlist ain't what you'd call above thinkin' of blackmail, to put it straight out. Course they don't know you, but they knows Arold Smiff. Me for the heather!"

"What did you think of the fight?" I asked him. "How did you explain it to them?"

"Hexplyne? To them barst—them blokes? I guv 'em fifteen quid apiece and all the loot they could find. What else 'ld they be wanting?" He grinned. "I might have cawst a few 'ints, such as that we was involved in a political move; the boys is hell on political moves. Maybe I mentioned the Sinn Feiners, careless-lyke. They drawed their own conclusions."

He squinted into his cup. "I think I shall call meself Jock MacSmiff," he said meditatively. "Ar, that's a good Scotch name. Maybe I'll even give up the gin. Take Scotch whisky instead, I mean. More patriotic, lyke."

"You'll be able to afford it, old chap, should you live to be a hundred," I told him. "It was nearly all your doing, yours and Geoff's, that we won our fight."

The waiter brought a bottle of Piper Heidsieck '43. The Colonel stood up to propose the first toast.

"Gentlemen and Marion, I give you ex-Sergeant Henry Johnson. There is only one thing we can say of him: greater love hath no man, that a man lay down his life for his friends."

WE drank standing. The waiter popped up with a second bottle. We resumed our seats, and Alec said, "The next is mine. I drink to the good green earth, and the race of men who live on it. Maybe they don't go about slopping over with gratitude for its beauty, but I think they appreciate it just the same, and I'm damned glad we saved it for 'em!"

Half-laughing, we drank that one, and many more. I drank to my Jaguar, now a deep red color and never to be identified with the sinister black car which flew out of Manchester that night so long ago. Doctor John drank to Jerry Wolfe, who first discovered the abominable race of beast-folk. Geoff toasted our army of rogues.

They all drank to our happiness, Marion's and mine. Then we called for a fifth bottle, and drank a tall glass down in memory of our victory, total and forever final, over the beast-folk of the silver land. I twirled my glass and stared at it, my eyes unfocused slightly, and I mused on *them*.

The usurpers...

Sir Lawrence Hockling, to give him his human name, had been as good as his word. Within a day, all through the land, the aliens had begun to decamp in disgust. As messengers raced behind the veil to tell their brothers the sad news, the exodus spread; first through the great centers of population, London and Birmingham and Sheffield, Cardiff and Liverpool, and thence into the countryside until all England was touched by this incredible mass desertion of a world, the beasts relinquished their stolen bodies and retreated into their own dimension. Well within my time limit of three days, the flight was completed. Some twenty-seven thousand robots were abandoned in the withdrawal.

Yet these puppets, these husks, had not died. They had become brainless, true; incapable of performing the simplest acts of caring for themselves; but they lived on. It was more horrible than their deaths would have been, I thought...and yet there was a ray of hope. I had talked it over with my friends, and they agreed there was a chance of its coming true.

These new things (one could no longer call them puppets, when the marionette-masters had gone) were like nothing on earth so much as newborn babies, babies in grown or half-grown bodies. What if their brains, unimpressed thus far by any experience, now began to develop, even as a baby's begins? What if they were not idiots, as they seemed to a horrified world to be, but simply newly-born humans who must be taught learning and manners and speech and all the rest, as though they were so many victims of a titanic wave of devastating total amnesia?

IF this were true—and it logically might be—then our rescue of the world would have been bought even more cheaply than we had calculated. Twenty-seven thousand amnesia victims to retrain is a damned sight better than that many idiots or, as we had expected at first, corpses!

There would still be sorrow and tragedy in the wake of the thing we had done. Couples who had spent lifetimes together had found themselves split, their mutual memories lost forever, as one turned infantile and looked mindlessly at the other. Men who had been forces for good in England (the usurpers were not intent on corrupting our daily lives, be it remembered, but on taking over our whole plane) had become useless hulks, great dribbling infants in old bodies. Many suicides had followed the plague of total amnesia.

Yet if my ray of hope chanced to be true, it took nine-tenths of the curse of the business off our consciences.

And some of the problems connected with the plague would then appear much smaller, and even rather funny; as for example, the twenty-seven thousand adolescents and adults who had never been housebroken...

Well! I came back to myself, filled up my glass again, and drank Arold's toast to Lord Nelson. How he ever crept into our party, I'm sure I don't know. By then, perhaps, we were all a little bit drunk; so we welcomed Lord Nelson, and drank to him joyously. Then we drank a final round to our long bitter fight with the usurpers, and we adjourned for the night. The next day we separated, each to his own place, and the great adventure was over at last.

CHAPTER TWENTY-FIVE

IT is just a year since we drove the usurpers out of England. (About the robots that they left behind, my hunch was right; for they are learning to take care of themselves, to walk and speak and act decently, and many have even begun to read and think again. When I consider this, I am inclined to go to my knees in thanks. What *might* have happened...!)

For a while I could not realize that my wild bluff had actually worked. I kept expecting a trick, a wholesale re-invasion of our world by the ogres. Even yet it is hard to comprehend. I suppose the only explanation is that all created things hate and fear death; in their fashion, the usurpers were just as scared of dying as the humblest human, and must have decided that the vicarious pleasures of earth weren't worth it.

Selfish fear gripped them, selfish deadly fear of murder in the dark. They shrugged themselves out of their stolen bodies, and abandoned the world they had hoped to conquer. The simplest of weapons, the easiest to employ, had done our work for us in a manner beyond our most optimistic dreams. The simplest weapon...fear.

Marion and I were married, of course, a year ago. The delirious happiness of our marriage has not cooled for me. Some day, perhaps, my feeling will have calmed to a steady, staid, cozy sort of affection; but not yet. Not for a long time yet.

I bought a little bookshop in Bury St. Edmonds, and took in Geoff and Alec as partners. It's the proper life for a quartet of reformed crusaders like the three of us and Marion. Peaceful, contemplative, and yet stimulating. We like it. And we like being together.

John is back on the seas as ship's doctor, the Colonel is laired up at the Albany, and Arold lives in Kirkcudbright, swilling great vats of Scotch whisky, I have no doubt. One day soon we must all get together for a grand reunion...

BUT a man cannot walk through fire without being burnt; and as there cannot be many such conflagrations as that through which I groped and fled and sought my way, it is only natural that my mind carries even yet a few scars of the burning. I do not expect—I dare not hope—that they will ever be wholly healed.

In certain moods, usually on dreary days when the sky is overcast and the sun is hidden, or sometimes at night when the great yellow hunter's moon rides in a black sky, the horror of the usurpers comes upon me with fresh and lurid obsession, more appalling than ever it was in the weeks of my hectic and headlong warfare. Then I go out into the streets or wander on the moorlands and fight with my hallucinations. A thousand times I tell myself that *they* are gone, that the world is clean and inviolate again; and a thousand times I hear in reply the hideous laughter of the fear that lives forever at the bottom of my soul.

I walk past a tavern, and see its door swing open, and catch a glimpse of the barman; and he seems to me in that moment to be, not a jovial red-faced fellow, but a twisting writhing monster shot with vivid lights and fringed with rippling pseudopods. A friend comes up behind to clap me on the shoulder, and I dread to turn and look at him, for fear of what he may be. I hear a snatch of speech from a wireless set, and the soft-cultured voice emanates, I believe in a sudden jolt of panic, from the lips of a marionette-creature controlled by a hellish and malevolent incubus.

So at last I take my terror home to Marion, and lose it in her arms...

THE END

If you've enjoyed this book, you will not want to miss these terrific titles...

ARMCHAIR SCI-FI & HORROR DOUBLE NOVELS, $12.95 each

D-11   **PERIL OF THE STARMEN** by Kris Neville
           THE STRANGE INVASION by Murray Leinster

D-12   **THE STAR LORD** by Boyd Ellanby
           CAPTIVES OF THE FLAME by Samuel R. Delaney

D-13   **MEN OF THE MORNING STAR** by Edmund Hamilton
           PLANET FOR PLUNDER by Hal Clement and Sam Merwin, Jr.

D-14   **ICE CITY OF THE GORGON** by Chester S. Geier and Richard S. Shaver
           WHEN THE WORLD TOTTERED by Lester Del Rey

D-15   **WORLDS WITHOUT END** by Clifford D. Simak
           THE LAVENDER VINE OF DEATH by Don Wilcox

D-16   **SHADOW ON THE MOON** by Joe Gibson
           ARMAGEDDON EARTH by Geoff St. Reynard

D-17   **THE GIRL WHO LOVED DEATH** by Paul W. Fairman
           SLAVE PLANET by Laurence M. Janifer

D-18   **SECOND CHANCE** by J. F. Bone
           MISSION TO A DISTANT STAR by Frank Belknap Long

D-19   **THE SYNDIC** by C. M. Kornbluth
           FLIGHT TO FOREVER by Poul Anderson

D-20   **SOMEWHERE I'LL FIND YOU** by Milton Lesser
           THE TIME ARMADA by Fox B. Holden

ARMCHAIR SCIENCE FICTION CLASSICS, $12.95 each

C-3   **INTO PLUTONIAN DEPTHS**
           by Stanton A. Coblentz

C-4   **CORPUS EARTHLING**
           by Louis Charbonneau

C-5   **THE TIME DISSOLVER**
           by Jerry Sohl

C-6   **WEST OF THE SUN**
           by Edgar Pangborn

ARMCHAIR SCIENCE FICTION & HORROR GEMS SERIES, $12.95 each

G-1   **SCIENCE FICTION GEMS, Vol. One**
           Isaac Asimov and others

G-2   **HORROR GEMS, Vol. One**
           Carl Jacobi and others